His-and-Hers Family

HELEN LACEY

MILLS & BOON®

For my dad, William Lacey
1926–1994
who taught me to love books and who I still miss every day.

First published in Great Britain 2013
by Mills & Boon, an imprint of Harlequin (UK) Limited.
Large Print edition 2013
Harlequin (UK) Limited,
Eton House, 18-24 Paradise Road,
Richmond, Surrey TW9 1SR

© Helen Lacey 2013

ISBN: 978 0 263 23760 3

Harlequin (UK) policy is to use papers that are natural,
renewable and recyclable products and made from
wood grown in sustainable forests. The logging
and manufacturing process conform to the legal
environmental regulations of the country of origin.

Printed and bound in Great Britain
by CPI Antony Rowe, Chippenham, Wiltshire

"My job is to protect her. Karen trusted me with that responsibility and I'll do it as best I can."

Fiona wrapped her arms around her waist and sat forward. "I won't screw this up. And I'll be whatever she needs me to be. There's no question about me trying to replace her mother. But I can be her friend."

"Yes, you can."

She let out a breath and experienced a heady warmth low down. There was something in his expression which heightened her awareness of him on every level.

She pushed some words out. "So, I guess considering you're her legal guardian, *we* should be friends, too."

Another look, longer, hotter. Hot enough to raise her temperature a degree or two.

"Logically. But I get the sense that whatever's going on here," he said and flicked a hand in the air, "it's got nothing to do with friendship."

"I don't think—"

"And everything to do with sex."

Dear Reader,

Welcome back to Crystal Point and to my second book for Mills & Boon® Cherish™.

If you've read my first book you might remember Fiona Walsh from *Made for Marriage*. Fiona is a kind-hearted, friendly schoolteacher who has settled in the small town to escape a painful past. But the secret she's kept hidden for fifteen years is suddenly a secret no more when businessman Wyatt Harper turns up and informs her that his teenage niece wants to meet her birth mother. Very soon Fiona comes face-to-face with the child she gave up for adoption when she was just fifteen, and finds herself falling for a man who has sworn off love.

I've had so many readers ask me when the bubbly yet very much alone Fiona will get her happy ending, and I hope you enjoy her journey and fall a little in love with Wyatt along the way. I also invite you to return to Crystal Point very soon.

I love hearing from readers and can be contacted via my website at www.helenlacey.com.

Warmest wishes,

Helen Lacey

HELEN LACEY

grew up reading *Black Beauty, Anne of Green Gables* and *Little House on the Prairie*. These childhood classics inspired her to write her first book when she was seven years old, a story about a girl and her horse. She continued to write, with the dream of one day being a published author, and writing for Cherish™ is the realization of that dream. She loves creating stories about strong heroes with a soft heart and heroines who get their happily-ever-after. For more about Helen, visit her website, www.helenlacey.com

Chapter One

It was the third time she had seen him in two days. And because she had a vivid imagination, Fiona Walsh had created all kinds of possible scenarios as to why the most gorgeous man she'd ever clapped her eyes upon appeared to be following her every move.

Who was he? An admirer? Lottery official? *Stalker?*

Yesterday morning she'd spotted him across the road outside her house, leaning on the hood of his car and speaking into his cell phone. She'd gone to collect her morning paper from the footpath and hung around by the gate for a few minutes, feigning interest in her wilted herb garden. Then he appeared by the foreshore that same afternoon while she ran her dog along the beach. Same car. Same kind of well-cut clothes. Same dark hair and superbly chiseled features.

Now he was at the riding school where she stabled her horse.

Fiona eased Titan, her Thoroughbred gelding, to a halt in the center of the sand arena and lifted the rim of her helmet. The man remained by his car, leaning against the door as he watched her. There was nothing threatening in his demeanor. He appeared more mildly curious than anything else. With the idea he wasn't about to attack her and toss her in the trunk of his car firmly out of her head, Fiona experienced a strange warmth across her skin. Handsome, nice car, the kind of clothes that oozed confidence—she couldn't help but be intrigued.

He was on his cell again, talking as he watched her. Fiona collected the reins and clicked Titan forward. The big gelding obeyed instantly, and she maneuvered him toward the entrance gate. No more guessing games. She'd find out who the man was and just what he wanted. Right now.

She dismounted and tethered Titan to the hitching rail. Once he was secured, she pulled off her riding hat and wasted a few seconds adjusting her hair. As she left the arena and walked purposefully across the yard, Fiona watched him end his call, slip the cell phone into a pocket and straighten to his full, broad-shouldered height.

Ten feet away she stopped and clipped her booted heels together. He was ridiculously good-looking and appeared to be in his early thirties. Even though sunglasses shielded his eyes, Fiona knew he was staring at her. She suddenly had a silly thought about her appearance and wished she'd worn something other than her grass-stained riding breeches and century-old T-shirt.

Silence stretched like elastic. Finally, she summoned the nerve and drew in a deep breath. "I guess you're not here to tell me I've won the lottery?"

He cracked a half smile and flipped the sunglasses off. "No."

She clamped her hands on her hips and tried to ignore the way her belly rolled over when she met his perfectly brilliant blue eyes. "Then why are you following me?"

"I'm not," he said and took a step toward her.

Fiona widened her gaze. "Three times in two days?" She clicked her fingers. "That's quite a coincidence."

"It's not a coincidence at all," he replied. "I've simply been waiting for the appropriate time to speak with you."

Fiona raised her chin as annoyance wove up her spine. He had a little too much self-assurance for her liking. "With me? What on earth for? I don't know you, and I—"

"Are you Fiona Lorelle Walsh?" he asked quietly, cutting her off.

She stilled and her breath grabbed at her throat. "What do you want?" she asked as suspicion crept along her skin.

He took another step. "To talk to you."

Fiona stared at him. He knew her full name? Who was he?

She had the urge to retreat. Get away. Put distance between herself and his lovely eyes. "I'm sorry, but I'm busy at the moment. I have to get back to my horse," she said and pivoted on her heels.

"Miss Walsh?" he called after her. "Fiona?"

She stopped midstride and took another breath, deeper, longer. Titan moved restlessly from his spot by the gate as though he sensed her unease. She spotted Callie Preston, owner of the riding school and her closest friend, walking across the arena toward the two remaining riders. If she needed her friend, Callie would be at her side in a moment. But she kept her wits. Whoever this stranger was, she wasn't afraid of him. Fiona turned around and faced the man behind her.

Her heart continued to thump madly. In the sunlight his hair appeared almost black and shimmered in a way she'd usually find attractive. But a voice told her not to think about him like that. "Who are you?"

"My name is Wyatt Harper."

She didn't recognize it. "What do you want?"

"To talk."

"What about?"

He stepped closer. "Perhaps we could go somewhere a little more private."

Fiona bristled. "This is plenty private."

He glanced toward the other riders and then back to her. After a moment he drew in a breath. "Okay. Firstly, let me assure you that I'm not any kind of threat to you."

Fiona didn't feel threatened. But her curiosity was at an all-time high. Sensing she needed every advantage she could get, she didn't quite let him off the hook. "I guess I'll know that when you tell me what you want." He smiled, and Fiona's insides gave a silly leap. "So, start talking."

He nodded. "Like I said, my name is Wyatt Harper." He pulled a small card from his shirt pocket and held it toward her.

She knew he stood still deliberately, allowing her the chance to move forward so he wouldn't appear intimidating. Smooth, she thought. And clever. She took a couple of steps, snatched the card and read it as she moved backward again. Sure enough, it said Wyatt Harper in bold print, with the title of managing director of Harper Engineering underneath it.

So, he had an impressive-looking job. It didn't explain what he wanted with her. "And?"

He met her gaze directly and took his time replying. "I'm here on behalf of Cecily Todd."

Cecily Todd? Fiona shook her head. "I don't know who that—"

"Cecily is my niece," he said quietly, interrupting her, "and the child you gave up for adoption fourteen years ago."

Her world quickly tilted on some invisible axis.

No. I don't believe it.

Oh, my God...is this happening?

She'd thought about this moment for years. Imagined it. Dreamed it and dreaded it. And her knees, usually rock-solid and strong, weakened like a bowl of jelly. Fiona bowed over fractionally as the air tried to squeeze into her lungs.

Breathe...just breathe...

He stepped forward but she raised a hand to warn him off.

"Take deep breaths."

He was clearly concerned but Fiona wasn't in any mood to be grateful. "Yeah," she huffed and cast him a sharp look. "No problem."

"Perhaps you should sit down," he suggested and looked around. "There are steps by the house. You could—"

"No," she said raggedly and gulped in air. "Please...just...stop."

He placed a hand on her shoulder. "I can't do that."

She grabbed her knees for support, took a deep breath and then straightened. He dropped his hand and stepped back. She drew in another steadying breath, trying to rally her strength.

"I'd like to talk with you about my niece," he said.

"Your niece?" she echoed vaguely, suddenly light-headed. Fiona put a hand to her temple. It was surreal. Dreamlike. As if it was happening to someone else, in some kind of alternate reality. "I feel a little woozy," she admitted.

He grasped her arm and this time she didn't ward him off. "Come on, you need to sit down."

She let him lead her toward the house. There were three steps, and he urged her to sit on the bottom rung. Fiona dropped her head between her knees. "I'm not normally like this."

"I surprised you," he said evenly. "I'm sorry."

"Surprised?" Fiona craned her neck to look at him. "You just shocked the hell out of me."

"What's going on here?"

She looked up. Callie stood twenty feet away. Her friend looked suspicious and regarded them seriously.

"It's all right, Callie," Fiona said. "I felt a little dizzy for a moment. I'm okay now."

"Who's this?" the other woman asked.

Fiona glanced at the man standing near her and saw his masked irritation at being spoken about in the third person. "Wyatt Harper," he said.

Fiona pulled her head up before her friend had

a chance to respond. "Thanks for coming over, Callie, but I'm fine now."

She didn't look convinced. "If you're sure..."

"I'm sure," Fiona said quickly.

She lingered for a moment, nodded and then walked off in the direction of the stables.

"Friend of yours?" he asked once she was out of earshot.

"Yes," Fiona replied. "She owns this place."

He nodded vaguely. "Are you really feeling okay?"

"I'm fine, thank you."

He nodded. "About Cecily, I wanted to—"

"Are you sure?" she asked, cutting him off. "I mean, are you sure she's...or that I'm her..."

"Her birth mother?"

She swallowed the heavy emotion in her throat. "Yes."

"If you're Fiona Walsh, then yes, I'm sure. I have documentation to support that you gave birth to Cecily."

She took a deep breath, drawing strength. "And you're her uncle?"

"That's right. My sister and her husband adopted Cecily."

A lovely couple. That's what she'd been told by the adoption agency. People who would be able to give her daughter everything she couldn't. Stability. Safety. A perfect home. She'd had fourteen years to imagine what they were like. Fourteen years where she hadn't known her child's name. Fourteen years to dream about reconnecting with the baby she'd given up.

But not like this. Not when she was totally unprepared and caught off guard. Whoever he was, and whatever he wanted, Fiona had no intention of falling apart in front of him. She didn't do vulnerable. Ever.

She stood and crossed her arms. The only words she could form came out. "Why now?"

He waited to respond, taking stretched-out seconds as he looked her over. "Because Cecily wants to meet you."

She shook her head instinctively. No one was going to turn her world upside down. Not ever again. She wasn't fifteen and gullible. She was nearly thirty and called the shots in her own life. If Wyatt Harper thought rocking up unannounced was going to give him an advantage, he could think again. *If* she had this conversation, she'd do it when *she* was ready, and not before.

"I can't do this here," she said and tilted her chin, defiant and with way more strength than she felt. "I won't. I need time to think. Goodbye, Mr. Harper."

"Fiona, you need to—"

"Goodbye," she said again and turned on her boots. She walked in a straight line back to the dressage arena and felt the sear of his gaze right up until she was out of view.

Minutes later she heard the sound of gravel crunching beneath tires. He was gone.

Fiona spent the following hour in a daze. She attended to Titan, got him untacked, fed and rugged, and headed home before Callie had a chance to question her about Wyatt Harper. She wasn't in the mood for an interrogation, not even from her closest friend.

Once she opened the door of her small house, dropped her keys on the hall stand and made her way to the living room, she let out an emotional shudder.

My daughter.

She sank down into the sofa.

My daughter's name is Cecily. Fiona had wondered so often what they'd called her. She hadn't had the strength to name her baby. It was better that way...that was what she'd been told.

The only way.

But how she'd despaired over her decision. Even knowing that at fifteen she hadn't been in a position to care for a baby and giving her up had been her only option.

The hardest decision I'd ever make.

That's what the nurses at the small country hospital where she'd given birth had said.

Your baby will be better off.

And then her great-uncle's voice, reminding her about her own mother.

The apple doesn't fall far from the tree.

Back then she'd believed him. Memories of

her mother, Shayne, were etched into her mind. Unreliable, self-absorbed, an irresponsible flake, more interested in staying out late and getting high than being a parent. A woman who'd forfeited her chance for an education at seventeen to raise a child she never really wanted, and who'd married a man she'd never loved. A marriage that had lasted two years. Tired of her life in the small town where she'd been raised and the rules she was forced to follow living in her uncle's house, Shayne packed up a then five-year-old Fiona and began following the rodeo circuit. She chased one cowboy after another, dragging Fiona through countless motel rooms and a string of transient jobs.

When she was fifteen, Fiona had been shipped back to her great-uncle…alone and scared and pregnant. Fiona had few illusions about Shayne. Her mother's reaction to her pregnancy was borne out of anger and resentment. Three weeks after Fiona was left at her uncle's farm, Shayne and her much younger rodeo-rider boyfriend were killed in a railway-crossing accident. She didn't grieve, didn't *feel*. There was too much hurt, too much betrayal, too much pain.

Six months later Fiona had given up her baby after only fifteen minutes of holding her. She'd said goodbye to her precious daughter and handed her over to strangers, hoping with all her heart that her baby would be treasured by her new family, knowing that because she'd agreed to a closed adoption she could never look for her, and lived on the hope that one day her daughter would seek her out. But she'd never really believed it. Never let hope linger for too long.

Until Wyatt Harper dropped into her world.

Her daughter's uncle. An envoy. Clearly here to check her out. Although, since he knew her full name, he'd probably done a fair amount of checking already. Fiona gripped her hands together. How much did he know? The paper trail was meager at best. With Shayne dead there was nothing linking Fiona to her mother's lover. Or what had happened on that terrible night.

Nothing except Cecily.

No one knew the truth. No one ever would.

Fiona had held on to her secret for over fourteen years. There was no mention of him anywhere. She hadn't talked about it since the day she was dumped on her uncle's doorstep. Her daughter's birth certificate stated father unknown. He was dead. What good would rehashing it do now?

Only…Wyatt Harper had turned up and she knew he'd have questions. *Questions I can't answer.* There would be no nice way to admit the truth about her daughter's conception.

So what did he really want? Did her daughter actually want to meet her? And if so, where were her adoptive parents? Why had Wyatt Harper been sent on this digging mission?

If she wanted answers, she had to pull herself together.

First, a shower and a change of clothes. And then a strategy. She liked strategies and lists and being organized. She didn't like being in the dark. She didn't like Wyatt Harper knowing things about her when she knew nothing of him.

She fingered the business card he'd given her. Seconds later she was at her computer and typed

Harper Engineering into the search engine. It wasn't long before she had a dozen or so hits. He was from the third generation of Harpers to run the steel-fabrication business. With well over one hundred employees at the huge factory on the outskirts of Sydney, he appeared to be doing everything right. There was a nice picture of him, too, with his father and grandfather. It was clearly a *family* business in the truest sense of the word.

Fiona flicked off the computer and headed for the kitchen. Muffin, her energetic Tenterfield Terrier, jumped up at the back door, and she quickly let the dog inside and fed her. The card in her hand burned her fingertips. There was only one way to find out what he wanted.

He'd failed. When he'd promised Cecily he wouldn't. Fiona Walsh obviously wasn't prepared to talk, and Wyatt felt as if the door had been well and truly slammed. She'd said she needed time—but time for what? She'd looked horrified when he'd faced her with the news.

Her pretty face had turned ghost-pale, emphasizing the brightness of her lips and sparkling blue-gray eyes.

He shouldn't have confronted her out in the open. Yesterday would have been better. But the moment he'd spotted her walking from her little house in her cute pajamas, he'd forgotten why he was there. Forgotten that he had a job to do and forgotten that Cecily was relying on him to *not* screw it up. But by the time he'd shaken the image of Fiona Walsh's bouncing hair and pretty face out of his head, she had disappeared inside.

Now, back in his hotel room, Wyatt had time to think about the way he'd ruined his chances. Cecily would be bitterly disappointed, and the last thing his niece needed was more of that. He checked emails and called his personal assistant. Glynis had been with him for ten years; she'd been with his father for twenty before that. The sixty-year-old widow was his right arm, sometimes his conscience and often his sounding board.

"Your flight is booked for tomorrow morning," she told him. "You *are* still coming back tomorrow, aren't you?"

"I'm not sure."

She made a disagreeable sound. "And Miss Walsh?"

"I've made contact. We'll see what happens." He wasn't about to admit he might have screwed up.

"Just be careful," she warned. "Sleeping dogs sleep for a good reason. Sometimes the past is best left where it is."

"It's what Cecily wants," he said and ended the call, feeling the weight of his promise to Cecily press between his shoulder blades.

When his niece had asked him to find her birth mother, Wyatt hadn't been surprised and he had understood her motives. Cecily wanted answers. Now that he'd met Fiona Walsh, Wyatt was intrigued and wanted some answers, too. He knew she was a teacher and had lived in Crystal Point for five years. Before that there had been a series of jobs at various schools, none lasting more than six months. She appeared to go from one small town to the next, never settling until now. What made Crystal Point different? Did she have roots in the small community? From the investigation he'd undertaken, Wyatt knew there were no relatives, only a great-uncle who'd passed away twelve months earlier and left her a modest inheritance after the sale of his property out west. There were no parents. No siblings. Not even a distant cousin she could claim as family.

Fiona Walsh seemed to be as alone as a person could possibly get.

She wasn't married...but maybe she had a boyfriend? She was as pretty as hell, after all. Her hair was an amazing color, not red, not blond but an unusual mix of both. In more normal circumstances, Wyatt would probably have been attracted to her.

Whoa...where did that come from?

He was here on Cecily's behalf. The kid had been through enough over the past eighteen months. Now she wanted to find her birth mother, and it was Wyatt's job to help her. He wasn't about to get caught up in Fiona's lovely blue-gray eyes. He wasn't about to rush into getting caught up with anyone, not after the disastrous end to his engagement eighteen months earlier. Yvette's betrayal had left a bitter taste in his mouth.

He knew he had to see Fiona again. He had to make her listen.

His cell rang and he picked up on the third ring. "Wyatt Harper."

"I'll meet you in half an hour."

Her husky voice was unmistakable. She'd called. Maybe he hadn't screwed up after all? "Great. Shall I come to you?"

"No," she said quickly. "I'll come to you."

Wyatt gave her the name of the hotel.

"Okay," she said. "I'll meet you in the foyer at five o'clock."

Then she hung up.

Fiona's drive into Bellandale took twenty minutes. The town was four hours north of Brisbane and had a population of sixty thousand. The streets were typically quiet for a Sunday afternoon, and she scored a parking spot outside the hotel. With her nerves severely stretched, she walked through the front doors and into the lobby.

There was no sign of him. She checked her watch. Three minutes to five.

Fiona ignored the concierge and headed for the lounge area in the centre of the lobby. There was a bar close by, and a waiter immediately approached to take her order. She declined and sank into one of the leather sofas. The foyer was eerily quiet, except for the faint sound of piped music and the occasion click of heels over the polished floor.

"Hello, Fiona."

She snapped her neck around. Wyatt Harper had approached and stood only feet away. Fiona did her best to overlook the way her traitorous belly flipped over. Okay...so he was good-looking and possessed the kind of body that was hard to ignore in his dark chinos and a white polo shirt. And he had great hair and glittering blue eyes. *Big deal*. The world was full of gorgeous men. And because this one had just dropped a bombshell into her organized little life, Fiona had every intention of ignoring the way her blood heated when he was within a six-foot radius.

"Hello."

He looked at her oddly and the heat intensified. Fiona pushed her hair back with shaking fingers, suddenly nervous of his scrutiny. Something flashed in his eyes. Approval? *Disapproval?* Did she look as if she was trying too hard with her sensible denim skirt, modest print blouse and even more sensible sandals? Maybe she should have put her hair up instead of letting it curl madly around her head? She bit at her lower lip to get rid of the lipstick she'd dabbed on.

"Thank you for coming," he said.

Fiona noticed the narrow black folder he carried. "I don't see the point in hiding from the truth."

He nodded, sat down opposite her and placed the folder on the low table between them. "So you acknowledge that you're Cecily's birth mother?"

Fiona inhaled. "I admit that I had a child fourteen years ago." She pointed to the folder. "You seem to have all the evidence that she's the baby I gave up for adoption."

"I do have proof," he said quietly. "Although one look at Cecily would be enough to convince you." He pushed himself back in the lounge. "She looks just like you. Same hair. Same chin. Same…" He looked at her mouth for a moment and Fiona's skin warmed. "Same color eyes."

She managed a brittle smile and twirled a lock of hair between her fingertips. "Poor kid got stuck with this color."

He watched her actions with blistering intensity. "She's very pretty."

Fiona's heart began to beat a little faster. She drew in a breath and asked the question that burned on the end of her tongue. "What does she know about me?"

Wyatt Harper's eyes darkened fractionally. "She knows you were young when you had her.

Cecily has always known she was adopted. My sister Karen and her husband, Jim, were open with her from an early age and supported her decision to find her birth mother when she was ready."

"And she's ready now—is that what you're saying?"

He nodded. "She began talking about finding you nearly two years ago. Karen and Jim planned to start searching but..." He stopped and took a moment. When he spoke again, Fiona heard rawness in his voice. "They were killed eighteen months ago."

Emotion she didn't understand clutched her throat. "I'm sorry," she whispered. "How did it happen?"

"They were rock fishing," he replied. "They got swept off a rock shelf. It was a crazy accident. They were mad for a dangerous sport and paid the price. When they died, that left Cecily—"

"Alone," Fiona said quickly and covered her mouth when she realized how it sounded.

"No, not alone," Wyatt told her pointedly. "She has her family. I was going to say that it left her with a lot to deal with. She handled it pretty well, considering. A few months ago, she announced she was ready to find you."

"She really wants to meet me?"

He nodded. "Yes, she does."

Her breath caught again. *My daughter wants to meet me.* Fiona got goose bumps. This was what she wanted…right? To know the child she'd given up. She had everything to gain from such a meeting. *Everything. Then why does the thought of it make me want to run?*

"When?" she asked and pulled herself forward.

"It's not that simple," he said quietly.

Fiona twisted her hands in her lap. "What do you mean?"

"I mean that Cecily has been through a lot, and as her legal guardian, I am going to make sure she is protected."

"From me?" she whispered and fought the rising annoyance. His responses were vague at best, and it irritated her no end. Fiona pulled her fractured nerves together. "I would never hurt her."

"Perhaps not intentionally. But I have to be sure about you. I need to be certain you won't do anything to jeopardize Cecily's emotional state."

Dumbstruck, Fiona glared at him with a mixture of disbelief and slowly gathering rage. His inference was insulting. But she quickly bit back her infamous redheaded temper. Getting mad with him wouldn't serve her. He held all the cards. And he knew it. "So what do I have to say to prove that I wouldn't do anything to upset her?"

He leaned forward and rested his elbows on his knees. "How about you start by telling me why you gave your baby away?"

Chapter Two

Wyatt knew he was out of line. She looked as if she wanted to slap his face. But he had to know what kind of person Fiona Walsh was before he'd let her into Cecily's life, no matter how much his niece wanted to know her.

It didn't help that she was so incredibly pretty his mind kept wandering.

"Isn't it in the file?" Her eyes darkened as she pointed to the folder between them. "I'm assuming that's some sort of report about me, about my life? If you've done your homework, you'd know that I was fifteen when I had Cecily and not in a position to care for a child."

"And your parents?"

"My mother's dead," she supplied. "But I guess you already knew that."

"Yes," he said. "I know your mother was killed in a train-crossing accident with her boyfriend."

"And you know the man she claimed was my father died when I was three years old."

"Claimed?" he asked.

She shrugged. "She married Eddie Walsh and I was born six months later. They only lived together for two years. I was told he disappeared and then died in a rodeo accident, although I'm not actually sure that's true. He could have skipped to avoid paying child support for all I know. What else do you want to know?"

There was enough bristle in her tone to make it clear she had a temper but was doing her best to keep it under wraps. "You're being very candid."

She raised a brow. "Isn't that what you want?

Answers…and an opportunity to see if I'm respectable and responsible enough to meet Cecily?"

"I don't—"

"And once you figure that out, Mr. Harper," she said, cutting him off without batting a lash, "you can answer *my* questions."

There's that temper.

Wyatt might have liked her to simply back down and agree to everything he said but he didn't really expect it. And he respected her spirit. "Wyatt."

"What?"

"My name," he replied. "It's Wyatt."

"Okay…*Wyatt*…so ask me another question. Ask me as many questions as you like."

He went for the most important. "Cecily's father? There's no record of him on the birth certificate."

"No record." Visible shutters quickly came up and it waved like a red flag. "That's right. It's what I wanted."

Wyatt pressed on. "Is there any chance he might make an appearance in her life?"

"No chance," she replied hollowly. "He's dead."

Dead? He hadn't expected that. "Who was he?"

"No one."

He immediately wondered if she knew *who* Cecily's biological father was, but didn't like how the question sounded rolling around in his head. "Does he have a name?"

"Since he's dead it really doesn't make any difference."

"Unless his family tries to have some claim on Cecily in the future."

"They won't," she said stiffly. "No one knows about him. My mother made sure of it."

Wyatt's interest grew. "She didn't approve?"

"What mother would approve of her fifteen-year-old daughter being pregnant?"

He nodded slowly. "You said you weren't in a position to care for a child? Did you mean because of your age or something else?"

"I lived with my elderly great-uncle," she said

stiffly. "My mother was dead. I was two years away from finishing high school. I had no income and no way of supporting myself or my baby."

It sounded like an impossible situation for a teenage girl. "If it's any consolation to you, Karen and Jim loved Cecily very much. They'd been trying to have a baby for a long time. Cecily brought them a great deal of happiness."

She smiled and the sparks in her eyes faded. "They didn't have any other children?"

Wyatt begrudgingly admired how she'd seamlessly moved the questions onto him. "Just Cecily."

"And you're her guardian now?"

"That's right," he replied. "Karen was the daughter from my father's first marriage and she was twelve years older than me."

She nodded fractionally. "So, you and your wife care for her?"

"I'm not married," he said but was pretty sure she knew that already from the look on her face.

Her expression narrowed. "Does Cecily live with you?"

"She spends most of her time at Waradoon, our family property in the Hunter Valley, which is just over an hour's drive from Harper Engineering. My parents are retired and my youngest sister still lives at home. Cecily goes to the local high school and is well settled. I have a place in the city but go to Waradoon most weekends. If not, Cecily visits me in the city."

"Why did they grant guardianship to you?"

He'd wondered it himself in the beginning. Neither Karen nor Jim had discussed what would happen to their daughter upon their deaths. Finding out he was named sole custodian of their precious child had come as a shock.

"Jim had no siblings and his parents are both in poor health," he explained. "My mother spends as much time with Cecily as she can. But my father is over seventy with a heart condition, my sister Ellen has a four-year-old and two-year-old twins, and my youngest sister, Rae, is twenty-five and in her third year of studying veterinary medicine."

"So you don't actually spend a lot of time with her?"

It was a pretty mild dig, but it annoyed him anyway. "I have a business to run and I get home when I can, which is usually most weekends. Cecily understands that. She also likes living at Waradoon. She has her horse there and her friends are close—"

"She has a horse?"

"Yes," he replied. "Something you have in common."

Wyatt stared at her, intrigued by the way her eyes changed color. He liked the coppery shine of her hair and the way it bounced around her face. He liked it a lot. And her perfectly shaped mouth was amazing. Something uncurled low in his abdomen, a kind of slow-burning awareness. He'd met pretty girls before. Prettier even. But he couldn't remember the last time a woman had attracted him so much and so quickly.

"So," she said after a moment. "What now?"

Wyatt forced his focus back to the issue. "That's up to Cecily."

He watched as her bottom lip disappeared between her teeth for a moment. "It looks like it's up to you."

"I'm not about to rush into this." In fact, Wyatt had no intention of rushing into anything ever again. If he'd shown that same sense less than two years ago, Yvette might not have had the opportunity to wreak havoc on his life and his family. "Although I understand how difficult that must be for you to hear."

"Do you?" she asked quietly.

Wyatt didn't miss the rawness in her voice. "There are a lot of people who risk getting hurt, and my primary job is to protect my niece." *And you.* He didn't say it, but the notion lodged firmly behind his ribs. He had what might be considered old-fashioned values…about some things. Maybe it came from having an older father. Whatever the reason, Wyatt wasn't about to start making decisions that had the potential to turn lives upside down, without thinking them through long and hard.

"Can I see that?" she asked and reached across to finger the edges of the folder on the table.

"Of course."

She slid it across her lap and opened the folder. Wyatt remained silent as she examined the contents. Her expression changed several times as she flicked through the pages, shifting from annoyance to sadness and then a kind of strained indignation.

"You've done your homework." She pushed the folder toward him. "You've got everything from a copy of Cecily's birth certificate to my sixth-grade report card. I hope you paid your investigator well for all the hard work."

Wyatt's spine straightened. "I needed to know who you were. Investigating your background was simply part of that process. I'm sure you can appreciate that."

"That's not who I am," she said as she grabbed her small handbag and stood. "That's a pile of paper."

Wyatt quickly got to his feet. "Then tell me who you are."

She glanced at the folder again. "I think you've already made up your mind. I think you know all about my childhood, you know my father ran off and that my mother was a junkie who couldn't hold down a job and never had any money in her pocket. I think you've read about how I've moved nine times in as many years. And I think you're wondering if I'm not just a bit too much like my mother and can't quite be trusted to meet Cecily and that I might taint her in some way."

She was close to the mark and he didn't bother denying it. "I have to consider what's best for Cecily."

"Yes," she agreed. "You do. But *you* came to *me*. You came to me because Cecily has questions about where she came from. I understand that. I know what it is to have an empty space inside. When I was fifteen, I was manipulated into agreeing to a closed adoption—forfeiting any hope I ever had of finding my daughter. I wasn't allowed to know anything about the people who had her. And then you show up with your nice smile and ultrapolite conversation and throw a few crumbs in my direction about the possibility of meeting my child." She took a shuddering breath. "Whatever your opinion of me, Mr. Harper, I won't be manipulated again or walked over. Now, if you'll excuse me, I need some time to consider what *I* want."

Without another word, she turned and strode away from him and out through the door. Wyatt stared after her through the glass windows, watching the way her hair bounced as she walked, suddenly mesmerized by the stiffness in her shoulders and the gentle sway of her hips.

He only let out a breath once she got into her car and drove off. Wyatt grabbed the folder and closed it. Nothing in the report had prepared him for that exchange. He'd expected…what? That she'd be so grateful to reconnect with Cecily she wouldn't put up any kind of resistance? That she'd be compliant and agreeable to everything he suggested or wanted? Right now he didn't know what to think. Had he scared her off? Did she actually want to meet Cecily? Fiona Walsh had gumption and he liked that about her. She wasn't a pushover. She was strong. He'd give her some time to settle into the idea, and then he knew he had to ask her straight out if she wanted to meet Cecily. Wyatt pulled his cell from his pocket. Glynis picked up on the third ring.

"Change of plans," he said.

"Which means?" his assistant asked.

"Cancel my flight for tomorrow."

There was a moment's silence. "I see. Do I re-book?"

"I'll let you know."

Glynis tutted. "How long are you staying?"

Until I fix this. "I'm not sure," he said and ended the call.

Fiona couldn't drag herself to work the following morning and called in sick. Which wasn't exactly a lie. She did feel genuinely unwell. Her head ached. Her heart ached. She never took time off. She kept herself in good health and loved her teaching job.

I just can't face all those happy little faces today.

She blamed Wyatt Harper for it, of course. Since he'd entered her life, she'd become an emotional mess. Crying...for Pete's sake, she never cried. When she opened the front door to Callie that afternoon, it took all her strength to not collapse in a heap at the other woman's feet.

"I was worried when the kids said you weren't at school today," she explained as she crossed through the door. "With good reason by the look of things."

Fiona sniffed and pushed up the sleeves of her dressing gown. "I'm sick."

Callie's perfect brows rose sharply. "Try again. And this time include what it has to do with that tall drink of water you were talking with yesterday."

Fiona hesitated for a microsecond. But this was Callie, her best friend and one of the few people she trusted, and the only person she'd told about her teenage pregnancy. "Remember how I told you I had baby when I was fifteen?"

Callie's eyes popped wide. "Absolutely."

Fiona quickly explained how she'd agreed to a closed adoption and who Wyatt Harper was.

"Are you sure he's telling the truth?" Callie asked once they were settled on the sofa, each with a coffee cup between their hands.

"Yes. He has Cecily's birth certificate and he says she looks just like me."

Callie looked at her over the rim of her cup. "Did you ask to see a picture?"

Fiona shook her head. "No…I wasn't sure I could bear seeing her photograph. In case I never get to see her for real. Does that make sense?"

Her friend nodded gently. "So what are you going to do about it?"

Fiona shrugged. "I'm not sure. That's to say, I'm not sure what *he's* going to do about it."

"You have rights," Callie said. "She's your child."

"A child I gave away. Wyatt Harper is the one with all the rights. He's her legal guardian. He's who her parents entrusted to care for her."

"But you said she doesn't live with him?"

"She lives mostly with her grandparents. But from what he said, I'm guessing they're a close-knit bunch. He runs the family business, and his parents are retired, so they'd have more time to look after her. His younger sister lives there also."

"Must be a big house."

"It's a hundred-acre property," she explained. "His father runs a small herd of Wagyu cattle—his mother dabbles in showing orchids. They're squeaky-clean and look like the perfect family."

"And he's what, thirtysomething and single and now a part-time parent to a teenage girl?" Callie rolled her big eyes. "Nothing is that perfect."

"He seems like one of those annoyingly self-sufficient men who can handle *everything*. I'm sure one little teenager wouldn't bring him down."

Callie smiled. "He is very nice-looking. Not that you'd ever be swayed by a handsome face."

"Er...no."

"Maybe you should see a lawyer?" Callie suggested. "I mean, he hasn't contacted you since yesterday—for all you know he's gone back to Sydney."

"I don't think so. He wanted something and he didn't get it. I don't think he's the kind of man who retreats easily, and I didn't exactly leave him on friendly terms." She smiled when she saw her friend's look. "Yeah, I lost my temper."

Callie's expression softened. "So, how do you feel about it? I mean, how do you feel about reconnecting with your daughter after so long?"

Fiona sucked in some air. "Confused and shocked. I always had hope but I tried not to get swept away with the idea of meeting her one day. It was too painful. But now it's a reality...and I'm scared. Because I'm still the person who gave her away." She expelled a heavy breath. "What must she think of me?"

Callie made a reassuring sound. "You were young—not much older than she is now. She'll understand once you explain. She's come looking for you, Fiona. That's a positive sign."

Fiona hoped so. But she had doubts. Reservations. What if Cecily didn't understand? What if all their reconnecting did was to upset her daughter? She didn't want that. Cecily had lost her parents, and Fiona didn't want to do anything that might add to her pain.

When her friend left about ten minutes later, Fiona, tired of looking like a washed-out rag, took a long shower. Once done, she finger-combed her hair, changed into comfy sweats and fed the dog. She had some assignments to grade and curled up on the sofa with her work and a fresh mug of coffee. She was about halfway through her pile of papers when Muffin started growling and rushed toward the front door after the bell rang.

When she pulled the door back, she found Wyatt Harper standing on the other side of the screen.

"Hello," he said casually, belying the sudden awareness that swirled between them.

She stepped back on her heels and ignored the way her heart seemed to be beating a little faster than usual. "What do you want?"

He held up a bag. "Dinner."

"I don't think—"

"For three," he said, cutting her off. "In case you have company."

"I'm alone," she said as her suspicions soared. "And I'm not hungry."

He raised both brows. "Are you sure?"

Fiona fought the impulse to close the door. She didn't want to be nice to him. But she wanted to know more about her daughter, and he was the key.

"You can come in." She stood to the side and allowed him to cross the threshold.

He wore beige cargoes and a black golf shirt, and she couldn't stop herself from checking him out. Okay, so the man had a nice body. She wasn't a rock. She was a perfectly normal woman reacting to a good-looking man. She wasn't about to beat herself up about it.

"Thank you," he said and walked past her. "Where do you want this?" he asked as he motioned to the bag in his hand. "Chinese. A bit of everything because I wasn't sure what you liked."

"The kitchen," she replied as she shut the door and then frowned as Muffin, the traitor, jumped up and down excitedly by Wyatt's feet, demanding attention. "This way."

He patted the dog for a moment before following her. When they reached the kitchen, Fiona stood on one side of the small square table and waited for him to take his place on the other side. She needed something between them.

She watched as he unloaded half a dozen small containers from the bag, then pulled out two sets of cutlery and a couple of serving spoons and grabbed two beers from the fridge. "Only light beer, I'm afraid."

"No problem."

Fiona placed everything on the table and scraped a chair across the tiled floor. "How did you know I'd be home tonight?"

He shrugged. "I didn't. I took a chance. It's a school night...and I figured you'd stay in."

Fiona pushed both beers toward him and he

disposed of the caps quickly. "Actually, I didn't work today." When he didn't respond, she explained. "I wasn't much good for anything after our conversation yesterday."

He pushed a beer back toward her. "That's honest."

"One of my many flaws," she said and took a small sip. "I have plenty. I often blurt things out before I think about what I'm saying. And I have a bad temper."

His blue eyes shone brilliantly. "Really?"

Fiona started opening the tops of the cartons and when she was done scooped a dumpling out of one of them with her fork. "Big surprise, huh?"

He grabbed a carton of noodles. "So, is there a boyfriend or significant other in the picture?"

She looked at him and colored beneath his penetrating stare. "Just me."

"Good," he said and piled food onto his fork. "More noodles for us."

Fiona was tempted to smile. There was a casual, easygoing way about his mood and she liked it. Too much. She didn't want to think about him *that* way. He was her ticket to her daughter, and she had to keep her head on straight. Imagining anything else was nonsensical.

"Wyatt…" She lingered over his name and discovered she liked the sound of it rolling around on her tongue. "What are you really doing here? I know it's not to share Chinese food or inquire about my love life."

He placed the fork on the small cardboard container. "I was concerned about you."

Fiona's skin tingled. "There's no need to be," she assured him. "I'm fine. I'm always fine."

"So you're fine?"

He was smiling at her, and Fiona experienced a strange dip low in her belly. Really low. She marshaled her wits. "So what have you decided to do about Cecily?"

He looked at her. "After our conversation yesterday, I thought it was more about what *you* wanted to do?"

I want to see her.

"I don't really know," she said instead. "I

thought I did. I thought I knew how I'd react if this moment ever came. Instead I'm completely unprepared. In my mind, when I played this moment over and over, Cecily was an adult and came to find me on her own. Then I could have faced her as an adult. But she's a child and I know I have to be the strong one…like I should know exactly how to respond and react. But I don't," she admitted. "Part of me is overjoyed. The other part…" She paused, waited and couldn't believe she was exposing her most vulnerable thoughts. "The other part almost wishes you'd never come here."

The air crackled as she waited for him to respond. "You are strong, Fiona. Anyone can see that. But I don't want you to have any illusions," he said directly. "Cecily wants this reunion—but she's a kid and at the moment is caught up in the excitement of the prospect of reconnecting with her birth mother. Once the dust settles and the novelty passes, the questions will start. And perhaps the blame. Are you ready for that?"

No, I'm not. She knew what questions would

come. But she wasn't about to admit that to the man in front of her. "Are you saying I *can* see her? That you approve of me?"

Wyatt wasn't sure what he was feeling. He'd read the investigator's report and could easily come to the conclusion that Fiona Walsh was a good person. She was a schoolteacher and had friends in the small community. Was it enough? She *seemed* suitable to connect with Cecily. But he'd been wrong before. And he couldn't be sure what Fiona intended, either, despite what she said. He knew what Cecily wanted, and that didn't make the decision any easier. She was as headstrong as they came, particularly on this issue. But there was bound to be fallout—and he didn't want his niece, his family *or* Fiona paying a heavy emotional price.

"I think…I think you'll do what's right for Cecily."

"I will," she said solemnly. "You have my word. My promise." She stalled for a second and then spoke again. "What's she like?"

"She's terrific. Cecily's a nice kid, but she doesn't hold back. She says what she thinks, blurts out whatever is on her mind and has a temper to match her red hair." His mouth flattened in a half smile. "Sound familiar?"

She nodded, and Wyatt saw her eyes shining just a little bit more than usual. "Do you have a picture?"

"Of Cecily? Yes," he said and took out his smartphone. He pressed a couple of buttons and passed it to her.

Silence stretched between them. Food and beer were forgotten. She blinked a few times and drew in a deep breath as she stared at the picture on the small screen. The resemblance between them was unmistakable, and Wyatt knew that seeing her daughter's image for the first time was difficult for her.

"Thank you," she said and pushed the phone across the table. "Can you send me a copy of that?"

"Sure." Wyatt popped it back into his pocket. "Have you any questions?"

"Hundreds."

He grinned and reclaimed his fork. "Fire away."

"Does she like school?"

"Yes. She's a good student."

"She has friends?"

"More than I could count."

She nodded. "Is she happy?"

"Most of the time. She struggled after Karen and Jim died. But with a lot of love and support, she pulled through. She's strong, gutsy." Wyatt watched Fiona's eyes shadow with a hazy kind of sadness. It twisted something inside his chest. Made him want to offer…*what?* Comfort? *Get a grip.* "She's a lot like you."

Fiona laughed. Brittle. Uncertain. "I'm not gutsy."

"I've read the file, remember?" he said and then wondered if mentioning it was wise. She didn't react and he decided to push deeper. "Why have you moved around so much?"

"Habit."

Wyatt's brows shot up. "That's not it. Tell me why."

She speared another dumpling and slid the carton across the table. "Looking for roots, I guess."

"Did you find them?"

She ate the dumpling, and when she licked her lips, his heart smashed in his chest. *I definitely have to stop looking at her mouth.*

"I found Callie and Evie, my two best friends," she explained. "And I like this town. I enjoy my job and my little house." She glanced around the room. "Plus I can have Titan nearby."

"So, no boyfriend?"

Her lips curled up. "Didn't we cover that already? I'm single."

"Happily?"

She stopped tossing her fork through a carton of spicy chicken. "Who's happy about being alone?"

She had a point. Although since he'd broken up with Yvette, Wyatt hadn't wanted to pursue anything serious with anyone. He'd dated one woman since then, and that had faded before it had really begun. He wasn't in any kind of hurry to lay his heart on the line again. He doubted he ever would be. "Better to be unhappy alone than miserable with someone else."

"Spoken from experience?" she asked.

He shrugged the question off. "Old news."

She swapped cartons. "You know things about me. It's only fair for you to share a little, don't you think?"

Wyatt grabbed the spicy chicken, took a bite and then washed it down with the beer. "I was engaged. It didn't work out."

"Do you miss it?" she asked. "Being with someone, I mean? Just belonging, having somebody to talk with, having someone who *gets* you?"

"My relationship with my ex-fiancée wasn't that romantic."

She frowned. "But you loved her?"

Nothing he said was going to get him away from Fiona's inquisitive gaze. "I guess."

He knew it didn't sound all that convincing. But he wasn't convinced he actually had loved

Yvette. There'd been attraction and a certain compatibility, sure...but love? It was a nice idea, but did it really exist?

"Did a number on you, did she?"

Pretty, smart and intuitive. "You could say that."

"At least you've had the courage to try," she said in between a mouthful of noodles.

"Have you ever been close?"

She shook her head. "Nope. I'm always the best friend."

"What?"

She smiled. "You know, the best friend. There's the girl who always gets the guy...and then there's the ever-faithful best friend standing on the sidelines. That's me."

The best friend. Who was she kidding? She made herself sound about as exciting as an old shoe. Ridiculous. When he could feel the vibration of her through to his blood. Her skin was as clear as a camellia flower, and that hair... He suddenly had a startling image of it trailing across his chest.

Wyatt cleared his throat and drank some beer. "I suppose we should talk about Cecily."

She looked up. "That is why you're here, isn't it?"

"Of course," he replied, choosing his words. "Before I agree to anything, I need to know if you *really* want to connect with her. Or if you feel ambivalent or like you have no other choice because it's what Cecily wants. If that's the case, believe me, I'll leave tomorrow and you'll never hear from me again until you're ready to make the next move."

Panic quickly filled her eyes. "No…don't do that."

Wyatt didn't respond. He waited. She had to make a decision. There were no acceptable half measures. Fiona Walsh was either in or out.

"I want…" She stopped, paused, took a long breath. He waited some more for her to speak again. "I do want this," she said finally, and Wyatt didn't miss the way her eyes glistened. "I want a chance to explain why I gave her up."

"And the hard questions?" he shot back. "Because she's going to ask them and you need to be ready."

"I will be."

Wyatt wasn't sure. Something was amiss; he felt it through to his bones. There was something she wasn't telling him. He pushed the food aside. "Fiona, about Cecily's father—I think there are things you're not saying."

She shook her head quickly. Too quickly. "There's nothing. He's dead. He can never hurt her."

Wyatt immediately picked up on her words. "Did he hurt *you?*"

Fiona's eyes fluttered. "I didn't mean that. I meant…I meant he's dead and won't ever be a part of her life."

"And that's all?"

She nodded. "That's all."

Caution rattled around in his head, but he stopped the interrogation. "Okay, I'll talk with Cecily when I get home. We'll work something out. Cecily's welfare is my priority, so you understand that any initial contact will be supervised?"

She nodded. "Of course. I'd like to write her a letter, if that's okay with you. There are some things I'd like to say to her, and I think a letter might be a good way to start. I'll understand if you need to read it before she does."

Her lips glistened and looked delicious, and Wyatt's libido took serious notice. "Sure. I'll text you my address." He pushed the beer aside. "I should probably be going. I have an early flight in the morning."

She stood up, and he lingered for a moment before he got to his feet. Suddenly, leaving didn't seem like such a great idea. Stunned to realize how much he enjoyed her company and wanted more of it, Wyatt remained by the table and stared at her. The air between them grew thicker, hotter, as though some kind of seductive force had blown into the room.

She was closer now, barely a couple feet away. Close enough to touch if he reached for her. His fingertips tingled at the thought.

"Are you all right?" she asked a little breath-lessly.

"I'm just…" He stopped. *I'm just thinking about kissing you.* "Nothing." He pulled the car keys from his pocket and rattled them. "Thanks for the beer."

"Thank you for dinner."

"No problem. I'll be in touch."

She smiled. "Well, good night."

"Good night, Fiona," Wyatt said and got out of there as quickly as he could before he forgot all the reasons why he shouldn't be attracted to her and did something really stupid.

Chapter Three

"So, what's she like?"

Wyatt had barely walked into the main house at Waradoon late the following afternoon when his mother corralled him with the question. He dropped his keys on the hall stand. "She's nice."

"Nice?" Janet Harper's silvery brows rose swiftly. "That's all?"

In no mood for the third degree, Wyatt uncharacteristically ignored his mother and headed for the big kitchen at the rear of the house. He grabbed a bottle of water from the refrigerator and tossed the lid in the trash.

"Yeah...nice," he said when he spotted his mother ten feet behind him, with her hands firmly on her hips.

"Have you agreed for her to meet Cecily?"

It hadn't been a difficult decision. He instinctively knew Fiona was a good person. Despite also knowing she was holding something back, his concerns were minimal. It was unrealistic to think she'd simply lay her life open because he wanted answers. He could wait. In time he'd know everything about her. He'd make sure of it. "Eventually. Once I've talked with Cecily about it."

"She'll be home from her riding lesson soon. And full of questions. She's almost jumping out of her skin over this." Janet's voice dropped an octave. "I hope this woman doesn't—"

"She has a name," he said quietly. "And don't stress—you'll like Fiona."

Wyatt wished he didn't like her as much as he did. He'd spent the past twenty-four hours thinking of little else.

And the fact I wanted to kiss her last night.

"Fiona," his mother echoed, and he quickly got his thoughts back on track. "Yes. And she's nice. So you keep saying."

Wyatt frowned. His mother had way too much intuition for his liking. "Stop smiling."

"I trust your judgment," she said and sat at the long table. "If you say she's nice, I'm sure she's exactly that. You'll do what's right for Cecily and the family. You always do."

Did he? He certainly hadn't when he'd jumped into his relationship with Yvette. He'd invited her into his family and paid the price. But Wyatt understood the meaning of his mother's words. He had every intention of ensuring Cecily's well-being. And he wanted to protect Fiona, too. As for the family, they were all curious about Cecily's birth mother, especially his sisters. He certainly wasn't about to unleash them on an unsuspecting Fiona.

"Uncle Wyatt! You're here!"

Cecily stood in the doorway dressed in her riding garb, and he was amazed how much she looked like her mother. *Not her mother. That was Karen. Her* birth *mother.*

She raced across the room and landed against him with a resounding thud.

He hugged her tightly. "Hey, kid, good to see you."

"You, too," she said on a rushed breath. "So, tell me everything. Did you see her, did you talk to her, does she want to meet me?"

"Yes, yes and yes."

Cecily's eyes filled with moisture. "Really? I can meet her. I can talk to her?"

Wyatt nodded. He knew Cecily was eager, but he also knew he needed to show caution and get her to take things slowly. "She's going to write to you. Once she's done that, you can make up your mind about what you want to do."

Cecily pulled back and straightened her shoulders. "I already know what I want, Uncle Wyatt. I want to meet her. And soon."

She gave a determined sniff and left the room to change and attend to her homework.

"I told you she was keen."

Cecily wanted to meet her birth mother. Fiona wanted to reconnect with the child she'd given up. If it worked out, everyone would be happy. But if not, Wyatt could see the potential for disaster.

"You know," his mother said in that way that meant he was supposed to listen, "you could take some time off and take Cecily to see *her*. It might be easier for Cecily to meet her birth mother away from Waradoon. I'm sure Miss Walsh would feel overwhelmed to come here with all of us hanging around, if that's what you were planning."

He wasn't planning anything. The logistics had been on the back burner. But bring her to Waradoon? Wyatt's focus had been on getting to know Fiona before he made any decisions.

And now that I know her, I can't get her out of my mind....

He paid his mother attention again. "You mean take Cecily to Crystal Point?"

"Why not? How long has it been since you've taken a vacation? And you know how Cecily loves the beach." Janet raised her brows. "It might do you some good, too."

He didn't miss the dig. "I don't need a vacation."

She clearly didn't agree and pulled no punches in telling him so. "Your father had his first heart attack when he was forty-two because he worked too hard. I don't want to see that happen to you. There's more to life than Harper Engineering."

Wyatt knew what was coming. He needed a life. He needed a wife. But that wasn't going to happen.

"The business will be—"

"Fine," she assured him. "Alessio will be there," she said of his brother-in-law and right-hand man. "Take a few weeks and—"

"A few weeks?" Wyatt stared at his mother. "I can't do that."

"Sure you can," she said and smiled. "School breaks up soon for two weeks. I don't think pulling Cecily out of classes for an extra week would hurt her."

A few weeks in Crystal Point? Cecily would

jump at the opportunity, he was sure. And Fiona…would she agreed to whatever he suggested if it meant having the chance to reconnect with her daughter?

I'm just not sure I should be spending three weeks around Fiona Walsh.

But other than sending Cecily to Crystal Point alone, which he would never do, or invite Fiona to Waradoon, which he wasn't sure she'd agree to, what option did he have?

"So it's all arranged?" Fiona asked her friend Evie Dunn.

"Yep," Evie replied. "They're booked to arrive on Saturday and are staying for nearly three weeks." Evie's black brows rose sharply. "You know, I've told you this at least four times already."

She knew that. But she wanted to hear it again. And again. Her daughter was coming to meet her. *My daughter is coming here.*

The reality was both exciting and terrifying.

Cecily had read the letter Fiona had sent via

her uncle and had quickly replied with an email, including photographs, and Fiona had choked back tears as she'd read her daughter's words. They'd been heartfelt and full of courage.

Fiona found herself holding her breath. "I know…just checking."

"Good thing we had that cancellation," Evie said.

Evie's bed-and-breakfast, Dunn Inn, was a popular retreat in the small town and usually had full occupancy. The cancellation of guests meant that two rooms were available, and Fiona couldn't have been happier.

"You're gonna be loco by the time they get here," Callie said and passed Fiona a drink. It was Friday night and the art class in Evie's studio was over. Two other participants had bailed ten minutes earlier, and it left Fiona sharing a drink with Callie, Evie and Evie's younger sister, Mary-Jayne Preston. They liked to think of it as Friday night cocktails, but with Evie only three months away from having a baby, they made do with peach iced tea instead of alcohol.

Only Mary-Jayne, or M.J. as she was called, complained. Fiona was happy to keep her mind buzzing.

"So, he's hot? The uncle?" M.J. asked in her usual boots-and-all manner.

"Yep. Hotter than Hades." It was Callie, who was married to Evie and M.J.'s older brother, Noah, who replied. "The original tall, dark and handsome."

Fiona sipped her tea. She wasn't going to think about Wyatt. Definitely not.

"And single?" M.J.'s eyes popped wide. "From a wealthy family and running a successful business? Interesting."

Fiona pushed aside the niggling resentment forming in her blood. It shouldn't matter to her that another woman might find Wyatt attractive...but it did. If she dared summon the courage, she would admit the truth—that she was nervous about seeing him again.

He'd emailed her with details of their upcoming visit, and Fiona knew she'd read, and then reread, each of his messages more times than was sensible. But Wyatt was hard to ignore, even through something as bland as an email or text message. Of course, there was nothing even remotely personal in his messages. They were only about Cecily. Which was what she wanted, right?

His indifference gave her the opportunity to focus on her daughter. She learned about Cecily's school, her friends, her beloved horse, Banjo, and the family who clearly adored her. Talking with her daughter seemed so natural and not awkward, like she had imagined for so many years.

Awkward she saved for Wyatt. And the stretched nerves she took with herself every-where she went—she saved them for him, too. And the fluttering in her belly whenever she thought about his blue eyes and perfectly sexy smile.

"Earth to Fiona?"

She snapped her thoughts back to the moment and discovered her three friends staring at her with raised brows and widened eyes. "I was thinking about Cecily," she said and took a drink.

"You sighed," M.J. told her. "Loudly."

"I cleared my throat," she said in defense. "So, who's up for more iced tea?"

Callie checked her watch. "Count me out. I have to get going. I promised Noah I'd be home early."

Fiona didn't miss the dreamy look on her friend's face. Callie adored her husband and four stepchildren. And with a pregnant Evie soon to marry Callie's younger brother, Scott, the two families were now intimately linked. Sometimes, when she watched them interact and observed the friendly rivalry and obvious affection the siblings felt for one another, Fiona experienced a sharp pain in her chest.

She'd never known family. Her great-uncle Leonard had done his best to provide her with a safe home after her mother dumped her on his doorstep, but he'd been a dyed-in-the-wool bachelor with old-fashioned morals and hadn't known how to handle a pregnant and emotionally fraught fifteen-year-old girl. He kept her fed and clothed and gave her a place to live—in his mind that was enough.

There had been no question about her keeping the baby.

The deal was done before she'd gone into labor. A married couple was taking her baby—that was all Fiona was told. The adoption would be closed. She could never contact her child.

But now I have my daughter back....

Well, she had a *chance* at least.

But she knew there were going to be challenging times ahead. Cecily would have questions, and she still wasn't sure how she would answer them. *And Wyatt?* She knew he'd be watching her every move and trying to discover her secrets. But even knowing that, Fiona held a seed of optimism in her heart. And when she returned to her empty little house a short while later, Fiona didn't feel half the loneliness that normally weighed down her shoulders when she opened the front door. She felt...hope.

Purple. Or as the woman behind him said in a chirpy tone, lavender. Wyatt had never been in a room that was so *pretty*. As he dumped his bag by the foot of the bed, the hostess told him the room was usually used by honeymooners and couples. Cecily was happily entrenched in the smaller room next door, a much more appealing space decorated in beige and white. This was too much.

The big bed was strewn with more pillows than he'd ever seen. He couldn't sleep in here, surrounded by flowers and purple cushions. And what the hell was the scent hitting his nose like a boxing glove every time he moved...*potpourri?*

"So, I'll let you settle in," Evie Dunn said cheerfully.

Wyatt didn't have a chance to object. The woman walked out of the room, and seconds later Cecily bounded through the door.

She wrinkled her nose. "Uncle Wyatt, it smells like a perfume shop in here."

That did it. "Let's switch rooms."

"My allergies," she protested. "And I've already unpacked."

Yeah, her three cases. One for every week they were staying in Crystal Point.

"Right, allergies." He forgot about the sickly sweet room for a moment. "Are you ready to go?"

Cecily nodded. "Yep. I don't know why we couldn't meet here?"

"The hotel is better," he said quietly. *Neutral.* It was what Fiona wanted.

"But Evie said we could use the front living room, and I—"

"You know the deal. Let's go," he said, gently cutting her off. Sometimes Cecily's exuberance was exhausting.

"Do you think she'll like me? Do you think she'll be disappointed?" Cecily popped out questions at a million miles per hour. "What if she—"

"Cecily—relax. She'll like you," he assured

his niece. "I promise. And where's all this sudden anxiety coming from anyway? You've been talking on the phone and by email for two weeks now."

"But this is face-to-face," she said in a rush of breath. "And that's way different."

Yeah...way different. The tension knocking inside his chest was inexplicable. He didn't ever get like this. But thinking about Fiona Walsh stirred his blood. And considering the circumstances, Wyatt knew it was out of the question to be attracted to her. He couldn't afford to be sidetracked by Fiona's pretty face and lovely curves. He'd been swept away by physical attraction before. He wasn't about to make that same mistake again.

He only had to look at Cecily to know he had to keep his head on straight.

"You're going to be a hit. Trust me."

"I do, Uncle Wyatt," she said and hugged him. "I want it all to work out so much. I want Fiona to like me, and I want to like her back, too."

"I'm sure you will," he assured her. "She's nice."

Cecily shrugged. "Well, she *seems* nice. But you never really know what someone is like at first."

Wyatt heard the waver in his niece's voice. "Cecily, are you having doubts about this?"

She quickly shook her head. "No…just nerves, I guess."

He didn't doubt Fiona would be feeling the same apprehension. "We can go home anytime you want. Just say the word."

"I don't want to go home," she replied. "Not yet. I want to try and see if we can be…I dunno… friends maybe."

Wyatt admired Cecily's maturity. But he'd make sure he was on hand if the pressure became too much for her young shoulders. "Okay. Then let's go."

He herded her out of the bedroom and down the hall. The drive into town took fifteen minutes, and by the time he parked the rental car and took the lift from the basement car park, they were only a few minutes away from their meeting time.

He settled Cecily in the foyer, on the same leather sofa where he'd met with Fiona a couple of weeks earlier. The place was quiet, and he was glad they'd have privacy and not be crowded out by the familiar faces of Fiona's friends, like at the B and B.

"Uncle Wyatt?"

He shifted his attention back to the moment. "Yeah, kid?"

Cecily's voice dripped with anticipation. "Is that her?"

He turned, and sure enough, Fiona was walking through the hotel doors. He hadn't forgotten how pretty she was, and seeing her again only confirmed that the sensation rumbling through his chest was attraction. She wore a green dress and her strawberry blond hair flowed loose around her shoulders. *Lovely.*

When she came toward them, his blood seemed to stop pumping in his veins. She stood before them, all eyes and expectation as she looked at Cecily, then him, then Cecily again.

"Hi," she said softly.

Wyatt answered quietly. "Hello, Fiona."

This is one of those moments, he thought, *when worlds collide.* Fiona's world, his world, now forever joined by the young girl who stood by his side, stepping back and forth nervously on her heels.

"Hello, Cecily."

His niece took a moment, as though unsure about speaking to the woman who had given her life. Wyatt knew she wasn't really scared. Cecily wanted this. And Fiona…he made out caution and uncertainty and plain old happiness in her blue-gray eyes. It was uncanny how alike they were. Same hair, same complexion, same spirited temper.

"Um…hi," Cecily said quietly. "Thanks for coming."

Fiona stepped a little closer, and Wyatt wished he could harness all his strength for a second and give it to her, so this moment could pass easily between them.

"I'm really glad you wanted to meet me... and...found me," Fiona said a little uncomfortably.

"Well, it was Uncle Wyatt who actually found you," Cecily replied with a small smile.

Fiona looked at him, and the tightness in his chest expanded. "I know he did," she said, then faltered a little before she spoke again. "So, how was your trip?"

"Good," Cecily replied. "Uncle Wyatt let me have the window seat."

Fiona laughed softly, and the sound vibrated through him. She looked nervous, and he discreetly touched Cecily's arm, urging her forward. It was awkward for a moment, until Fiona smiled again and opened her arms slightly. Cecily stepped forward, and within seconds mother and daughter were together, hugging close, clearly emotional. Wyatt watched their exchange and swallowed the lump tightening his throat.

Fiona looked at him over Cecily's shoulder and smiled. Tears hung on her lashes and her eyes grew huge. Seeing her so vulnerable, so raw with joy and glowing with a kind of radiant happiness, made his insides hurt. Cecily was crying, too. There was no sadness, no regret. Just new feelings, new dreams, new hope.

And he knew instinctively he'd made the right decision in coming to Crystal Point. It was right for Cecily to meet her birth mother. All he had to do was get a handle on the growing attraction he had for Fiona.

Easy...yeah...right.

Fiona experienced such acute and all-consuming love as she held her daughter in her arms for only the second time in her life. Images of the baby cruelly snatched away within minutes of her birth, which up until this moment were the only memories she had, suddenly faded.

She looks like me....

Wyatt was right.

Wyatt...

Her heart rolled over as she looked at him. So tall and strong and handsome. It seemed right having him near. It gave her strength knowing he was only steps away. His closeness gave her courage to hold on to Cecily and let all her pent-up feelings rise to the surface.

"Let's sit down," she suggested and linked her arm through her daughter's.

"Why don't I leave you two alone for a while?" Wyatt said once they reached the sofa.

Fiona watched as Cecily stepped toward him. "No…don't go."

He sent his niece a peculiar look and then glanced toward Fiona. Something shimmered between them, and Fiona suddenly longed for his reassurance. And Cecily clearly wanted him on hand. "Cecily's right," she said and tried not to be wounded by the fact her daughter was unsure about being alone with her. "I'd like you to stay for a while, too." She looked at Cecily. "Okay?"

Cecily nodded. "Yes. Uncle Wyatt's cool."

Fiona didn't miss the affection in Cecily's words. She was undoubtedly attached to her uncle, who had taken over the role of parent. "I'm sure he is."

He grinned fractionally and sat down on the other sofa. Fiona relaxed and turned all her attention to the girl sitting beside her. Cecily was remarkable, and pride, pure and simple, surged through her blood and across her skin.

This is my daughter...my child... I made this exquisite creature.

Whatever happened from this moment, Fiona knew she would treasure the memory of Cecily's small hand clasped within hers. Regret and shame tapped at the back of her mind, but she wasn't about to let those kinds of thoughts invade the precious moment she was sharing with her daughter.

They talked for an hour, about everyday things. Cecily asked when she could see where Fiona lived and when she could visit Titan. They talked about their dogs and Cecily's friends.

"Nan and Pop are great," she said excitedly. "I can't wait for you to meet them. Auntie Rae knows everything about horses, and Auntie

Ellen is so good with kids. She's got twins and they're really cute. She lets me help with them when I stay with her and Uncle Alessio. He's Italian. And his family is superrich. Not that she married him for his money… He's really good-looking, too."

Fiona waited for Cecily to take a breath and stole a glance at Wyatt. He was smiling, silent and intense as he regarded them.

"If it's okay with your uncle, maybe we could go see Titan this afternoon?"

"Can we, please?" Cecily begged Wyatt as she got to her feet.

He nodded. "If you like."

"I'll go get my boots," her daughter said eagerly. "They're in the car. I'll be back in a minute," she said once Wyatt handed over the car keys.

She left the foyer like a whirlwind and headed for the elevators.

Once she was out of sight, Fiona looked at Wyatt. "She's incredible."

"She certainly is," he agreed. "A pocket dynamo. But adorable."

"She loves her family a lot," Fiona said without envy and ridiculously conscious of his powerful stare. "And you especially."

"It's mutual," he replied. "She's a great kid."

She looked toward her feet. "I guess she'll have a lot of questions?"

"Yes," he assured her. "But she probably won't ask them straightaway. She doesn't want to scare you off."

Her gaze darted upward. "I don't scare easily."

"Are you sure?"

His mouth twisted in such a sexy way Fiona's breath rushed out. "Positive," she replied and wondered if they were still talking about Cecily. The air seemed uncommonly warm.

"Cecily is smart and mature for her age. She's had to be," he said quietly, and Fiona picked up on the strain in his voice. "She wants you in her life—although in what capacity I'm not sure. I don't think she quite knows herself. Meeting you is the first step. From here it's up to you both to work out what kind of relationship you'll have."

"With you standing on point to make sure I don't mess it up?"

He shrugged. "My job is to protect her. Karen trusted me with that responsibility, and I'll do it as best I can."

Fiona wrapped her arms around her waist and sat forward. "I won't screw this up. And I'll be whatever she needs me to be. There's no question about me trying to replace her mother. But I can be her friend."

"Yes, you can."

She let out a breath and experienced a heady warmth deep in her belly. There was something in his expression that heightened her awareness of him on every level. It was futile to deny it— Fiona got a look from his glittering blue eyes that said he was as aware of her as she was of him.

She pushed some words out. "So, I guess considering you're her legal guardian, *we* should be friends, too."

Another look…longer, hotter. Hot enough to raise her temperature a degree or two.

"Logically. But I get the sense that whatever's going on here," he said, flicking a hand in the air, "hasn't got anything to do with friendship."

"I don't think—"

"And everything to do with sex."

Chapter Four

Not one usually lost for words, Fiona stared at him. Of course, it was the truth. But put out there, it sounded dangerous. Dangerous because she wanted to focus every ounce of her attention on her child.

Falling in lust, or anything else, was absolutely out of the question.

"Cecily is…"

"Our priority," he said, finishing her sentence. "Exactly. The last thing we should do is complicate that."

"I agree."

"So, whatever this is, we'll ignore it?"

She could do that. For Cecily's sake. For her own. "Absolutely."

He stood up abruptly and Fiona's pulse raced. In jeans and a navy shirt, he looked so good it was sinful. His broad shoulders, solid chest and well-cut arms were undeniably worth a long look. Everything about him screamed *sexy*. Everything. And Fiona's libido raced up to smack her around the head, yelling, *I'm here and what are you gonna do about it?*

Nothing…a mutually decided nothing.

Besides, she had a disastrous track record when it came to men.

She'd had a few lovers. And no one since Russ Daniels had bailed on her over two years earlier. Of course, Fiona had expected him to walk. *I always expect them to walk.*

And they never disappointed.

If they weren't walking out the door, they wanted to be just friends. She wasn't sexy. She wasn't beautiful. Pretty at best. Cute. Perky.

Friendly and funny and exactly the kind of woman who made a great *gal pal*.

And Wyatt Harper would figure that out soon enough.

"I'm back!" Cecily announced as she bounded across the foyer, riding boots dangling from one hand.

"Great," Fiona said as she got to her feet. "Let's get going." She looked at Wyatt. "You are coming with us?"

He looked as though gears were grinding around in his head and he was quickly calculating his next move. "No."

Fiona bit back her surprise. *He trusts me.* "Oh, I thought—"

"You can drop her back to the B and B when you're done, okay?"

Of course it was okay. "I'll make sure she's returned by five o'clock."

He nodded slowly. "See you then."

"We could all have dinner together?" Cecily suggested, clearly forgetting her earlier reluctance about being alone with her. "So we can celebrate. What about here?"

Wyatt spoke. "I'll see what I can do."

Cecily hugged him before they left, and Fiona fought the sudden urge to do the same. She had an inkling those arms would feel wonderful wrapped around her.

Instead, she smiled, said goodbye and turned on her heels.

The few hours she spent alone with Cecily were some of the most precious in her life, and Fiona knew she would treasure them always. As expected, her horse-crazy daughter fell in love with Titan. The big chestnut Thoroughbred gelding was primed and in show condition and looked magnificent beneath the glow of the warm winter sun.

"Banjo has a problem with his pedal bone," Cecily explained with a frown. "So he's not suitable for dressage. But soon," she said as she buried her face in Titan's neck and inhaled the beloved horsey scent. "Uncle Wyatt says he'll buy me a new horse soon. Of course, I'll keep Banjo as a companion pony." She rubbed her small hands down the gelding's shoulder. "My aunt Rae will help me find the right horse. Or…" She lingered over her words for a moment. "Or maybe you could?"

Fiona's heart contracted. "I'd like that."

Cecily looked at her. "It's funny, don't you think, that we both have a horse? Like a sign or something. Do you believe in signs?"

"I do. Very much so."

"Uncle Wyatt says it's just coincidence."

He would. "Well, he seems like a practical type of person. It's good to have different points of view."

Cecily smiled. "That's what he says, too."

Uh-oh. She didn't want to keep finding commonality with him. That was more dangerous than thinking he was the most gorgeous thing on two legs. "We're both right, then. So, do you want to go to my house and meet Muffin?"

Cecily checked her watch and it made Fiona

smile. Excited, passionate about life and incredibly sensible. She loved that about her daughter.

"I guess…for a while. But we have to be back by five o'clock."

"I remember," Fiona said and linked her elbow through Cecily's.

Twenty minutes later, Muffin was a big hit. Cecily was in the kitchen of her little house, scratching the dog behind the ears. "She's cute. I like your house."

Fiona smiled. "It's small compared to what you're used to."

Cecily shrugged. "I guess. Waradoon is huge. My real house was sort of midsize."

"Your real house?"

Cecily met her gaze. "Where I lived with my parents." She went quiet for a moment. "They were good parents, in case you were wondering. I mean, I was happy most of the time."

"Most?"

Cecily immediately looked as if she wished she hadn't said the word. "I meant I was happy, that's all. I loved my parents a lot. My mother was always there for me...." She stopped and glanced down to her feet. "My dad was funny and told really bad jokes."

There was a sting in her daughter's words. But Fiona didn't press her. Wyatt had warned her to expect some resistance. As much as it hurt, she had to allow Cecily her feelings. "I'm glad. And it's okay living at Waradoon with your grandparents now? Your uncle told me he gets back every weekend?"

"That's right," Cecily replied quietly. "Uncle Wyatt is good at looking after me."

"I figured that."

"And he's not all serious and worried about me as though I'm going to fall apart or something like Nan and Pop. Not all the time anyway. Pop's been really sad since my mother died."

Fiona's throat tightened. "He lost his daughter. It will take time for him to stop being so sad."

"I guess." Cecily stroked the dog some more and stared toward the floor. "Did it...did it take you a long time...I mean, when you lost me?"

But I didn't just lose you. I gave you up. I

abandoned you. Her heart contracted in a vise-like grip. "Forever," she admitted and was relieved when Cecily looked at her.

"I guess you didn't have much choice, you know, when you decided about the adoption thing?" she asked, then immediately looked as if she wished she hadn't. "That's what Uncle Wyatt said."

Fiona remembered what Wyatt had said about Cecily not wanting to scare her off with too many hard questions too soon, and she swiftly tried to put her at ease. "It was a difficult time. And I'm really happy that you have a nice family who love you."

"I do," Cecily assured her, and then a little firmer, "They really love me. And Uncle Wyatt is the best."

Fiona nodded. She was starting to realize that herself.

Wyatt hadn't any idea how he was supposed to fill his time while Cecily and Fiona became acquainted. After making dinner reservations at the hotel, he drove back to the B and B but refused to hang out in the ridiculous purple room. Instead he grabbed his laptop and headed for the kitchen. Evie Dunn was in residence, baking something that smelled so good his stomach growled.

"Coffee?" she asked when he entered the room.

"Sure. Thank you."

She passed him a mug. "There's milk in the refrigerator."

Wyatt declined. "This is fine," he said, then asked politely, "When's your baby due?"

She patted her expanded belly. "In three months."

"Congratulations," he said and drank some coffee. He remembered Fiona telling him Evie was getting married soon.

Evie smiled. "Thank you. You know, it's good of you to allow Fiona this time with your niece."

"It's what Cecily wants."

"And Fiona."

What *did* Fiona want? He immediately wondered and his thoughts had nothing to do with

Cecily. He knew it was foolish thinking about her in any way other than Cecily's birth mother. Cecily was the priority. The kid had been through the emotional wringer, and he wasn't about to do anything that might upset her. Specifically, acting on his attraction for Fiona.

He'd get over it.

"She's a good person."

Wyatt looked at Evie. "I know."

Evie's dramatically arched brows rose. "She's more fragile than she likes to make out."

He wasn't about to disagree. He also wasn't about to get into a discussion with this woman, who was obviously a close friend of Fiona's. Wyatt was struck by a sudden surge of loyalty toward Fiona. "I know. So, is there someplace I can get internet access?"

She gave him a look, a half smile and then let him off the hook. "The study is the second room off the front hall—help yourself."

Wyatt grabbed the coffee and laptop and left the room.

As promised, Fiona returned Cecily at five

o'clock. Wyatt had spent a couple of hours in the office, made a call to Alessio to discuss a new contract acquisition and sent a few emails. His niece took no time in telling him what a great afternoon she'd had and how Fiona owned the most beautiful horse on the planet. He switched off the computer and swiveled in the high-backed leather chair.

Fiona stood in the doorway. She smiled at him and Wyatt's insides crunched. He cleared his throat. "Dinner's all set. I'll pick you up at six-thirty." Cecily nudged his shoulder. "*We'll* pick you up."

"Sure. Thanks. I'll see you later, Cecily."

Wyatt remained seated and watched as his niece hugged Fiona.

Once she had left, Cecily perched herself by the desk. "Well?" he asked.

She nodded. "I like her."

"And?" he prompted.

Sometimes mature beyond her age, Cecily looked every one of her fourteen years as she bit her bottom lip. "And nothing. I like her. She's nice, just like you said. Do you think I could ask her about my father?"

Wyatt wasn't sure. Fiona had been vague at best about the man. He had told Cecily her biological father had passed away, and his niece had accepted the news with quiet acceptance. But she had questions only Fiona could answer, and he wasn't convinced Fiona would tell the truth. He sensed she was hiding something from him—something that wasn't in the investigator's file. And knew he had to find out what it was and decide if it was something he wanted Cecily to know about.

"Maybe you should take some time getting to know her first?" he said. "Relationships take time."

Good advice. Pity he didn't take it when he'd jumped into his engagement to Yvette.

She shrugged. "I suppose. But I really want to know about my father. And my grandparents and any other relatives I had. Do you think she regrets giving me up?"

Wyatt chose his words carefully. "I imagine she'd have some regrets."

His niece drew in a deep breath. "She did say she was glad I had a nice family. I didn't know what to call her, though," she admitted, and Wyatt immediately reached out and grabbed Cecily's hand, squeezing it tightly. "The idea of calling her Fiona feels weird…but it's not like she's really my mother or anything."

"Maybe you could ask Fiona what she thinks about that?" he suggested gently. "You could come up with a name together—like a nickname?"

Cecily's eyes widened dramatically. "That's a good idea." She nodded, smiled and hugged him quickly. "Thanks, Uncle Wyatt. I'm going to get changed."

After lingering at the desk for another five minutes, he shut the computer down and headed back to the purple room. He showered in the en suite bathroom and changed into fresh clothes. Cecily tapped on his door at six-twenty as he was clipping his watch onto his wrist.

"How do I look?" she asked as she flounced into the room and twirled, showing off wide-legged jeans covered in sparkly diamanté. "Too much?"

When it came to Cecily's fashion sense, she had her own style. "You look great. Come on, let's go."

She laughed and bounded ahead as Wyatt grabbed the keys to the rental car.

The drive to Fiona's house took only minutes, and the sun was setting as he pulled into the driveway. He saw her silhouette pass by the window. The outline of her curvy body was unmistakable as she moved, and the way his insides rolled over simply thinking about her forced Wyatt to sit in his seat for a long moment after he'd switched off the engine.

"Uncle Wyatt?"

Cecily's voice turned his thoughts around. "Yeah?"

"Are you okay?"

"Sure," he said and sucked in a breath and

opened the door. "Jump in the backseat and I'll be just a minute."

By the time he reached her front door, Wyatt felt as if he was sixteen years old and picking a girl up for a date.

But this is not a date.

Fiona pulled the door wide as he tapped on the frame. "Hi," she said. "I'm ready."

Stupid, he thought, to imagine she would be as uncomfortable as he was. Except something about her demeanor got his attention, and he knew, without a doubt, she was experiencing the same spike in awareness. The little black dress she wore, which fell over her hips and showed off all her lovely attributes, didn't help. "Cecily's waiting."

She smiled, flicked off the light from inside the doorjamb and shut the door. "Like I said—I'm ready."

Wyatt was ready, too...ready to take her in his arms and kiss her beautiful mouth.

He stood aside and let her pass. Once inside the car, Wyatt did his best to ignore the flowery scent of her perfume, which hit him with lightning force every time she moved. The drive into town was only made bearable by Cecily's endless chatter.

He parked the car and they headed up and within minutes they were being seated in the restaurant.

"Champagne," his niece insisted to the hovering waitress once they sat down.

Wyatt shot her a *no chance* look. "Wine," he said and picked a bottle from the list. "And one raspberry lemonade," he added to the smiling attendant before she walked away.

Cecily heaved a dramatic sigh. "Uncle Wyatt," she complained. "This is a celebration. How can I celebrate with soda?"

"Easily," he replied. "I'm sure Fiona understands." He looked at her for the first time since they'd been seated. He wasn't sure why, but he wanted her to think him responsible and a good fill-in parent for Cecily.

She nodded and he appreciated the unity. "Soda will work just as well," she said and touched Cecily's hand. "So let's order because I'm starving."

Their drinks arrived, and once they ordered food, Cecily insisted on toasting to being reunited with her birth mother.

"To new beginnings," Fiona said quietly, and as they clinked glasses, Wyatt didn't miss the glitter of moisture in her eyes.

"To family," Cecily said and grinned.

The tears Fiona had valiantly tried to suppress tipped over.

But they were happy tears. She *was* happy. Being with Cecily filled her heart in places that been empty for so long. The years of being afraid her daughter would reject her had faded because Cecily had accepted her into her life. Fiona admired her daughter so much.

Her gaze flicked to Wyatt. *This, on the other hand, is where it gets complicated.* In all her life she couldn't remember any man having such a potent effect on her. But with Cecily bouncing in her seat beside her, Fiona knew having feelings for Wyatt…any feelings…was completely out of the question. She remembered what he'd said about logic and sex. Logical was out. It was illogical to want him. Not when she had such a disastrous history in relationships and not when Cecily was bound to be caught in the middle when she failed to hold his attention for longer than a moment. As for sex? She didn't do casual. She didn't have sex with men she hardly knew.

Only, on some level, she felt as if she did know Wyatt and that he knew her. Looking at him, sharing molecules of space with him, she was inexplicably drawn toward the awareness thrumming through her entire body.

I really want him….

And worse.

I really like him….

They chatted about ordinary things, and once dinner was served, Cecily stopped talking and ate with gusto. She had a healthy appetite and it made Fiona smile, counting all the ways she and her daughter were alike.

"More wine?" Wyatt asked as Fiona speared the stuffed chicken breast on her plate.

She nodded, afraid to speak because her mouth was dry and cottony.

"Can we go shopping sometime this week?" Cecily asked her uncle between mouthfuls of fettuccine.

"Sure," Wyatt said as he poured. "For anything in particular?"

Cecily gave him a big grin. "Well, I was thinking about Christmas in July."

He frowned. "What?"

"You know—a Christmas celebration in July. Auntie Ellen was telling me about it. Apparently lots of people do it."

He didn't look convinced. "What people?"

Cecily made a face and looked at Fiona. "Christmas is always a big deal at Waradoon," she explained and played with her fork. "I thought it would be nice to celebrate it now, since we've missed out on so many real Christmases together. What do you say, Uncle Wyatt?"

The holidays had never been a particularly

cheerful time for Fiona growing up. Shayne had rarely remembered to celebrate the event and her uncle had been too busy running the farm to be bothered with a tree or gifts. Since she'd settled in Crystal Point, Fiona usually spent the day with Callie or Evie and her family. Things had changed now Callie was married. And since Evie's wedding to Callie's younger brother, Scott Jones, was only a couple of months away and their baby was due a month after that, Fiona wasn't sure she would fit within the Preston fold anymore. She'd be the outsider, like she had been so many times before. But she would do anything to see happiness radiating on her daughter's face.

"I think it's a great idea," she said and smiled at her daughter. "I'll put up a tree."

Cecily laughed. "That would be cool. We can get gifts and put them under the tree." She turned to her uncle. "Now you *have* to take me shopping so I can exactly the right gift for Fiona."

"Okay," he said.

"And we should go, too," she suggested to

Cecily, and her heart flipped over when she saw her daughter's infectious smile in between another mouthful of pasta. "I'm sure you want to get something for your uncle."

Cecily giggled. "Ha—he's already got everything he wants."

Fiona looked at Wyatt and burned hot and dizzy beneath his stare as the awareness between them sizzled.

"Not everything," he said evenly.

She took a long drink and focused her attention on her meal. Was she imagining how highly suggestive his words sounded? She didn't dare look at him. Didn't dare let herself get caught up in his brilliant blue eyes.

Fiona inhaled deeply and started a conversation about horses, clearly Cecily's favorite thing. "We could go riding together," she suggested. "Callie will have a horse you can borrow while you're here. Of course, as long as your uncle says it's okay."

"I'm sure you'll keep her safe," he said as he looked at her over the rim of his glass.

As she met his gaze, Fiona was struck by how handsome he was. She'd never been one to be swept away by good looks. But he had his own brand of magnetism, which was quickly becoming impossible to ignore.

"Of course."

Cecily nodded happily and excused herself to use the bathroom. Once she was out of sight, Fiona picked up her glass and pretended to drink her wine, acutely conscious of the heat between them.

He pushed the plate forward. "Would you like to spend tomorrow morning with Cecily?"

"I'd like that," she said and smiled. "I appreciate that you trust me with her."

"I wouldn't be here if I didn't. But you should know that Cecily has questions for you," he explained. "You were expecting questions, right? She wants to know about her father, her grandparents...your family."

I don't have a family. Only Cecily...

Panic set in behind her ribs. Of course she knew questions would come. "I'll tell her—"

"What?" he asked. "I'd like to know exactly what you plan to tell her. I'd like to know what wasn't in the investigator's file."

He knew everything about her life—at least, he thought he did. No one knew about the man who'd taken her innocence. Not the nights she'd been left alone in motel rooms while Shayne chased one cowboy after another. Or the hunger from entire days without food. No one needed to know that. Especially not Cecily. But the questions about her father weren't going to be avoided easily. Especially when Wyatt had made it clear he wanted to know, too.

"He was…a friend," she said, thinking it wasn't exactly a lie. Jamie Corbett had been her mother's lover and someone Fiona had trusted… until the night Shayne had left them alone together in their shabby hotel room.

"A friend?"

"Yes. And like I said, he's dead. Talking about him won't change that."

He shifted in his seat and looked at her. "Is there something you're not telling me?"

Panic wound up her spine. Okay, so he could see right through her. It wasn't really surprising. She was vulnerable around Wyatt. Her attraction to him had been steadily building, like a rising tide. Spending time with him increased those feelings. If she were to keep her secret safe, Fiona knew she had to avoid being alone with him and concentrate on Cecily.

"I've told you everything I—"

"I'm back!"

Cecily's announcement silenced Fiona immediately. "Good. We were just about to tuck into the rest of your fettuccine."

The smiles all around belied the tension now ingrained in her bones. She feigned interest in her dinner and concentrated on not looking at Wyatt for the rest of the evening.

They left about an hour later, and by the time he pulled the car up outside her house, Fiona was a bundle of nervous energy. Cecily was dozing in the backseat and muttered a weary-sounding goodbye as she listened to her iPod. Before Fiona could protest, Wyatt was out of the car and had opened her door. Chivalrous, too, she thought with an inward groan. And handsome and so sexy she could hardly breathe as she stood beside him and walked toward the front door. The tiny porch seemed even smaller with his six-foot-something frame now standing by the door.

She fumbled with her keys and felt his closeness like a cloak. The dim glow of the overhead light created a heady intimacy. The white shirt he wore amplified the broadness of his shoulders and narrow waist. Warmth crept along her skin, followed by a lightning bolt of lust. But Cecily was in the car barely meters away, and Fiona knew she shouldn't be having such thoughts.

"Would you like me to do that?" he asked. "You look like you're having trouble."

Fiona pushed the key in the lock. "No, it's fine. Well, good night. Thank you for dinner."

He watched her with burning intensity. "I'll drop Cecily off tomorrow so you can spend the day together."

"Okay. I appreciate your—"

"Good night, Fiona," he said and dipped his head to kiss her cheek.

She shouldn't have sucked in a sharp breath. She shouldn't have felt as though her knees were going to give way. *It's just a kiss on the cheek, for heaven's sake.* But she did. And worse, a sound, half moan, half groan, rattled low in her throat. She knew he heard it because he smiled against her skin.

When he pulled back, he was still smiling. *Like he knows I want him.*

"Good night, Wyatt."

He headed down the three steps and took a few strides. Before Fiona had a chance to push the front door on its hinges, he turned. "Hey," he said quietly to get her attention.

Fiona drew in a breath. "Yes?"

He gave her such a sexy smile and she was quickly intoxicated. "You know, you look really good in a dress."

As he drove off, Fiona slumped against the door.

I will not like him.

Too late.

Chapter Five

"Tell me about the kid."

Fiona turned from her spot in Evie's kitchen. It was day three. The past forty-eight hours had been wonderful. Even better, she hadn't been in a position to spend any time alone with Wyatt. There had been no more questions, no more inquisitions. Cecily had asked about her father and for the moment had accepted Fiona's brief acknowledgment of the young man who'd been a rodeo cowboy and had been killed in an accident. She didn't mention the part about him being her mother's much younger lover. Or how he'd forced sex without her consent. There was an ugly word for what happened, but Fiona didn't like how it sounded on the edge of her tongue. Cecily didn't need to know the violent details of her conception.

Fiona had arrived at Evie's bed-and-breakfast at eleven o'clock and found Cecily and Evie's son Trevor shooting hoops near the studio at the side of the house. Evie was in the main part of the house with her other guests, and Fiona had taken over making sandwiches in the kitchen.

And now Wyatt stood framed in the doorway, dressed in jeans and a T-shirt, glaring at her.

"The kid?" She raised her brows, took her hands off the kettle and tried not to think about how her knees turned weak. She grabbed a tea towel and covered the plate of wrap-style sandwiches she'd made. "Trevor? He's Evie's son."

He nodded. "He's been monopolizing Cecily all morning. You know, I didn't bring her here so she could get mixed up with some—"

"Relax," Fiona insisted when she realized where the conversation was heading and that

Wyatt looked ready to punch someone in the nose. "Trevor's a nice boy. Sensible and trustworthy."

"Like all teenage boys, right?"

She stiffened and gripped the countertop. "Like he's been raised to be by his mother, who is my friend." Fiona grabbed a mug and poured coffee into it. "Here, drink this and calm down."

"I don't want to calm down," he said as he strode into the room. "I want to know that my niece is—"

"She's perfectly fine," Fiona said, taking no interest in his scowl or the fact he clearly didn't like being interrupted or pacified with caffeine. "She's shooting hoops, not smoking a crack pipe. And she's having fun with someone her own age."

"It's the kind of fun that concerns me."

Fiona suppressed a smile. "What, they don't have teenage boys where you're from?"

He didn't like sarcasm, either. "You're not helping."

"What exactly do you think she's going to

get up to?" she asked and pointed to the coffee again. "She's a sensible girl. She won't do anything foolish."

"Even sensible girls can get into trouble."

She didn't miss the meaning of his words. So there it was, out between them. And to his credit, Wyatt immediately looked as though he wished he hadn't said it. But out was out. And Fiona had no intention of pretending otherwise.

Besides, being annoyed with him helped her stop imagining him naked. Which she'd done with alarming regularity over the past few days.

"She's not me. And I've never claimed to be sensible."

"I shouldn't have—"

"Don't," she insisted. It didn't matter what he thought. She wouldn't let it. One silly kiss on the cheek didn't make them...*anything*. "I'd expect you to have an opinion. You've read the file. You know everything, right? The hopeless mother, the father who didn't want me, the countless schools. I wasn't exactly the poster child for a normal life." Fiona crossed her arms and drew air deep into her lungs. "But when I look at Cecily, when I see what an incredible girl she has become, I could never regret any of it. If I did that would be like saying I wished she'd never been born…and imagining a world without Cecily in it would be impossible to bear."

As speeches went, this was right up there. Right up there with making him feel like a complete jerk. Wyatt huffed out a breath and sat down. "I apologize. I'm not usually so clumsy."

She actually laughed. "I'd bet you've never had a clumsy moment in your life."

Except around you. He didn't say it. And didn't want to start thinking about why she affected him as she did. "I'm not about to start judging you, Fiona. If I'm acting like an overprotective parent, it's because I have no idea what I'm doing."

She came around the bench and settled her hips against the counter.

Wyatt tried to not think about how good her legs looked stretched out from the short skirt she wore. He had a hell of a time thinking about anything else when she was so close.

One brow came up. "You were surprised they granted you guardianship?"

"Yes," he replied and wondered how she seemed to know what he was thinking. "My sister three years younger is married with her own children so I assumed Karen would believe that Ellen and Alessio would have been the better option."

"I think they made the right choice," she said quietly. "Cecily thinks you've hung the moon, so you're off to a good start."

"I don't want to screw it up for her sake. She's been through enough."

"You won't," she assured him. "It's been eighteen months since her parents passed away and she's happy and healthy."

Wyatt bit back a laugh. "I'm not sure if that has anything to do with me."

"You'd be surprised. In my experience, as a teacher," she qualified, "I see children from different backgrounds and situations, single parents, foster parents, grandparents, two-parent families, and they're all doing the best they can. The thing is, Wyatt, no one gets it right every time."

He knew she was right, and her words offered the kind of comfort he'd somehow forgotten existed. "Do you mean like thinking every teenage boy who so much as looks at her is after something?" Spoken out loud, it sounded ridiculously paranoid.

She nodded. "Exactly. I wouldn't encourage her to be friends with Trevor if I thought he couldn't be trusted. You didn't expect Cecily to spend every minute of her holiday with either of us, did you?"

"I'm not sure what I expected," he said candidly, suddenly wanting to kiss her so much his whole body was on high alert. "I didn't expect…"

She stilled. "What?"

"I didn't expect I'd be this…" Wyatt stopped, pausing to consider if admitting anything was wise at this point—when they both knew it couldn't go anywhere. But for the past few days, he'd been going quietly out of his mind thinking about her. "I didn't expect I'd be this attracted to you."

Fiona sucked in a breath. *Okay...what now?* "Me, either."

Not the most sensible response. Not even close. "Inconvenient, then?"

She nodded. "Very."

"Is avoiding me helping any?"

Fiona rubbed her hands down her thighs and didn't miss the way his eyes followed her every move. "Not so far."

Something hot and seductive swept into the room. It toyed with them for a moment, tracing the edges of the building awareness, and she experienced a surge of longing so deep, so intense, her knees threatened to give way.

"Fiona..."

How he came to be in front of her she wasn't sure. She vaguely heard the chair being scraped back. There were no other sounds. Only her heart beating madly. Only some faraway voice telling her to stop whatever was about to happen.

"Wyatt...we can't... It's not..."

"I know we can't," he said softly.

Fiona said his name again. Anything more wouldn't come. When his arms moved to either side of her, trapping her against the counter, it merely intensified the desire scorching her skin, her blood and her very bones. She tilted her head back to look at him and recognized the raw hunger in his blue eyes.

She drew in a soft breath, waiting, feeling the heat between them rise like a coiled serpent. Her lips parted, anticipating his kiss. And wanting it. When he touched his mouth to hers, every ounce of lingering resistance disappeared. There was nothing else. Only feeling. Only his kiss. Only Wyatt.

She reached up and laid her hands on his shoulders. He was solid, strong, just as she'd expected. She'd been kissed before, had experienced desire before. But never like this. He leaned into her and continued to kiss her mouth, slanting his lips over hers with gentle provocation.

Whoosh...

She'd heard about it, read about it, secretly dreamed of one day finding someone who would make her feel so alive.

It's only lust.

Powerful, heady and electrifying. Exactly what it should be. But the warning voice in her head prevailed.

It's only sex.

And sex wasn't enough to sustain anything other than a brief, forgettable relationship. She knew that. But as his tongue gently wound around hers, for one crazy moment it felt enough. The fact he wasn't touching her in any way other than the kiss was incredibly erotic to her senses. Nothing rushed. No quick hands. No hasty gratification. No demands. This was slow and seductive and captivating, and he coaxed a response she gave willingly.

When the kiss was over and he lifted his head, Fiona kept her hands where they were.

She looked up, met his gaze and knew her lips quivered, knew he'd see every scrap of desire brimming in her eyes.

"Not a good idea?"

She swallowed hard. "No."

He pulled back and straightened. "You're right. It won't happen again."

It seemed like a monumental promise. Too big. Too much. Something neither could hold to. He wanted her. She wanted him. But it wasn't enough. Cecily was too important. "You're right...it won't."

"I should back off."

"Yes, you should."

He stepped aside and put space between them. Luckily, because just then Cecily and Trevor bounced through the back door, laughing loudly as they bundled into the room.

The kiss was forgotten, and Fiona caught Wyatt's sudden disapproving look when he saw Trevor and she frowned at him. He got the message and immediately switched to a smile so fake she almost laughed out loud. When the kids said they wanted to go to the beach, his pasted-on smile looked frozen onto his handsome face.

"Lily's going to be there," Cecily announced.

Lily was Callie's stepdaughter and Trevor's cousin. Fiona had introduced them the day before, and the girls, almost the same age, had hit it off immediately. The fact it was winter didn't seem to put the kids off going swimming. The weather was mild and she knew the water would be bearable. "As long as your uncle says it's okay."

He didn't waste any time saying, "We'll go with you."

Fiona didn't miss the inclusive *we,* and Cecily's startled expression stood out like a beacon. "You hate the beach."

"We'll all go," he said, firmer this time, and Cecily clearly knew not to argue the point. Once the kids left to change into their swimsuits, Fiona turned to Wyatt. "Don't like the beach, huh?"

"In the middle of winter? Not particularly."

Fiona grinned. "City boy," she teased. "So why are *we* going?"

"I like teenage boys even less."

Fiona sighed heavily. The man was as stubborn as they came. "Trevor's a good kid. Didn't we already go over this stuff?"

He shrugged. "Humor me anyway."

"Doesn't look like I have a choice." She moved around the bench and flicked the kettle switch. "I just have to get brunch into the front dining room for the guests and then I'm all yours."

Probably not the best way to put it. The words smacked of innuendo. Wyatt raised a brow and got rid of the fake smile. "Can I help?"

"Are you good in the kitchen?"

He smiled in a sexy way. "I know my way around."

She didn't doubt it. If he was good in the kitchen, she didn't dare imagine his skill in the bedroom. "I've got it," she said and grabbed the sandwiches. "I'll meet you outside in fifteen minutes."

He nodded and left the room.

Fiona's fifteen minutes turned into twenty-five. By the time she headed outside, Wyatt was pacing the front driveway.

"Sorry," she said breathlessly. "Just had to let Evie know we're heading off." She looked around. "Where are the kids?"

"Five minutes ahead of us."

He let them go unsupervised? "I'm impressed."

"I'm trusting your judgment."

"Smartest move you've made today." She took a few steps and then turned back to face him. "Well, let's go. Don't want that five to turn into ten."

She crossed the road and headed across the grassy stretch toward the pathway that led to the beach.

Wyatt caught up with her in mere seconds. "It's what, a ten-minute walk?"

"About that," she replied as he came beside her. "This path leads down toward the patrolled beach in front of the tourist park. You remember the beach, don't you? You followed me down there once."

"That first day—I remember."

She grinned and forgot that she should be jumping out of her skin to avoid enjoying his company. "Stalker."

Wyatt laughed and the sound vibrated through her. He was so easy to be with. Easy to like. The sound of waves crashing along the shoreline and the scent of wild jasmine in the air created a relaxed mood between them. That kiss would usually have put her on high alert. Strange that it didn't. Strange that all she wanted to do was keep talking with him. And kiss him again. *And kiss only him for the rest of my life.*

"Why aren't you married?"

His question quickly shoved her back into the moment. "I told you already."

"Because you're always the best friend. Yeah, right. What's the real reason?"

She shrugged. What could she say? Men weren't exactly lining up for her. The ones that had always found her lacking in some way. Of course, Fiona knew why. She had too many secrets. Too much baggage. Things she couldn't tell.

"I've never been in love," she said and felt the

truth of her own words through to her bones. "So what about you?" she asked, determined to shake him off the subject of her loveless love life. "How come your engagement didn't work out?"

He didn't falter a step, although Fiona sensed his reticence. "We were incompatible."

"That's a good shot at avoiding the question without giving a real answer."

He flicked sunglasses on. "I worked long hours. She didn't like it."

"Being committed to your job isn't exactly a deal breaker. What's the real reason?"

The woman was relentless, Wyatt thought and tried to not think about how much he longed to take her hand in his. He couldn't recall the last time he'd wanted to do that. Maybe never. He felt ridiculous even thinking it. Stupid and foolish, he knew it was inappropriate. But as he walked with her beneath the late-morning sun and remembered how sweetly she'd kissed him, Wyatt experienced an odd tightening in his chest. Because it felt as if they were…what?

Courting.

He almost laughed out loud.

People didn't do that anymore. He didn't do that ever. Sappy, romantic notions had never been his thing. He was practical and pragmatic. He worked hard, played fair and believed a man was measured by his integrity and how he treated others. Pretty girls with nice smiles didn't turn his head and make him forget he had a job to do. Reuniting Cecily successfully with her birth mother was his job, and he'd promised his niece he'd do everything he could to ensure it worked out. Karen and Jim were gone and he'd played his part in that. *He'd* suggested they take a break and work on their marriage. Little did he know that advice would send them to their deaths. He owed Cecily a chance to have a mother again, and he wasn't about to screw it up for her.

"Wyatt?"

He glanced at Fiona and the truth tumbled out. "She slept with someone else."

The pathway rounded a corner, and she stopped

at a narrow bridge crossing just before the tourist park. "I'm sorry."

He shrugged. "It happens."

"I guess. Doesn't make it hurt less, though."

Was he hurt? Wounded, maybe. And angry.
And disappointed that he'd been so blind about
Yvette. Wyatt was also man enough to take
some responsibility for what had happened between them. He'd jumped into their relationship
quickly, and he wasn't about to make that mistake again. Wyatt liked Fiona. And desired her.
But Yvette's betrayal made him wary and suspicious. He barely knew Fiona and couldn't be sure
her attraction to him was genuine. It seemed
real. It felt real when she'd kissed him. But his
ex-fiancée had pretended to care for six months
before he'd found her out. How could he be sure
Fiona wasn't using the attraction between them
to get closer to Cecily? He couldn't.

But still, she was smart and pretty and sexy.
The whole package. Exactly the kind of woman
Wyatt imagined he'd want. There was no out-
ward pretense with Fiona Walsh. There was a

deep earthiness in her manner, a kind of sweet honesty. Sometimes blunt, always sincere... just...*lovely.*

"I'm sure you will."

She looked at him oddly. "You're sure I will what?"

"Fall in love."

She half smiled and the air between them crackled. "I'm not holding my breath. Although Cecily has already hit me up for a little brother or sister one day."

"Really?" Wyatt wasn't really surprised, though. He knew his niece didn't relish being an only child. "Karen and Jim wanted to give her everything," he explained as she began walking again. The rise to the beach was ahead, and when she trudged up the sandbank, Wyatt followed.

She moved back and grabbed his arm. "I wasn't criticizing them."

Wyatt placed his hand over hers and rubbed his thumb over her fingertips. "I know that.

Cecily was the only child in the family for a long time so I guess we all indulged her."

"Your sister and her husband didn't try to adopt again?"

"No. They'd tried to have a baby for a long time before Cecily came into their lives. Jim had been working up north for several years when they started adoption proceedings. Actually, they were only three weeks away from returning to the Hunter Valley when Cecily became available."

She stiffened and tried to pull her hand away. He held on. "That didn't come out right."

"It's the truth," she said on a heavy sigh. "I gave her up. I let her go. She was *available*. I didn't get a say in which family she went to. My uncle and your sister insisted on a closed adoption, and I was so upset I agreed without really considering what it would mean—for me or my baby."

Her pain struck him hard between the ribs. "Karen should have—"

"I don't blame her," Fiona said quickly. "In her

shoes, I might have done the same thing. I was told what I needed to hear—that my baby had gone to the perfect couple."

Perfect? Wyatt fought the urge to set her straight. Instead, he remained loyal to his sister. He owed Karen as much. "They loved Cecily dearly."

"Then I guess I was right to let her go."

"Fiona, I want—"

"Hey!" Cecily's voice, loud and excited, crashed through the moment.

Wyatt dropped Fiona's hand and watched his niece climb up the small sand hill. She had a towel wrapped around her waist and water dripped over her bare feet. "Enjoy your swim?"

"Yeah." She laughed. "The water's cold, and Lily and I dunked Trevor. So…" She raised her eyebrows and looked at them both, grinning broadly. "Wanna explain why you guys were holding hands just now?"

"We weren't really—"

"No," he replied the same time Fiona started to protest. Wyatt knew better than to give in to

Cecily's curiosity. The kid had all the tenacity of a terrier.

She laughed again. "Hah—you're so busted."

Fiona moved forward, clearly mortified. "Well, I'm going over to the surf club to check my roster. I volunteer for beach patrol," she explained and looked quickly toward Cecily. "Have fun in the water—if it's too cold, don't stay in for too long. And swim between the flags."

She walked down the sand and headed back onto the path and into a nearby building. Once she was out of earshot, Wyatt turned back to his niece. "Was that necessary?"

Cecily gave a cat-who-got-the-cream grin. "You're the one caught making out, not me."

He frowned. "We were not making out," he said and got a powerful flashback of kissing Fiona in Evie's kitchen. "I was helping her up the sand bank."

They both knew it sounded like the lamest excuse they'd ever heard.

And Cecily had no compunction in telling him

so. "You know, I'm not a little kid. I'm okay with it if you like her. I like her, too."

"The reason we're here is so *you* can get to know Fiona. That's all."

"I get that," she replied and pulled her hair from its band. "All I'm saying is that if you want to take her out sometime, I wouldn't mind." Her eyes widened. "You could take her back to that restaurant we went to and get one of those tables in the corner where it's quiet and I dunno…romantic."

I am not standing here getting dating advice from a fourteen-year-old.

"And you can ditch whatever silly ideas you've got going on in your head and get back to your friends."

Cecily rolled her eyes. "Chill out, Uncle Wyatt. You are old enough to date, you know."

She skipped off back down the embankment, and Wyatt remained where he was until he saw her regroup with Trevor and Lily. Once assured she was safe, he stepped down the bank and headed for the building where he knew Fiona was hiding out.

* * *

"What's this?" Fiona asked Cameron Jakowski as she looked over the beach-patrol duty roster. "No Saturday shifts for the next three weeks?"

Cameron, full-time local police officer and part-time lifeguard, smiled and shook his head. "That's right."

Fiona settled herself on the other side of the counter. The surf club had two levels, and she was on the bottom floor where the lifeguards hung out when they weren't patrolling the beach. "Are you sure?"

"Positive. Enjoy the time with your daughter."

Of course he knew about Cecily. Cameron was Noah Preston's best friend, just as Callie was her best friend. Callie was married to Noah; it was natural Callie had told her husband about Cecily. And Fiona liked Cameron. They'd been friends since she'd first settled in Crystal Point. They'd even dated a few times. But there was no chemistry between them and their relationship was completely platonic.

"Thank you. You're a gem."

He grabbed her shoulders and squeezed. "I know. So, is Cecily going to Lily's sleepover this Saturday?"

"Absolutely. Now that Cecily and Lily are firm friends, I haven't a chance of keeping them apart."

Cameron laughed and hugged her tighter. At precisely the same time Wyatt rounded the doorway. He stopped, stared and didn't look happy about what he saw. Not one bit.

Chapter Six

There was suddenly enough raw testosterone in the room to make up a football team. Fiona extracted herself from Cameron's brotherly hug and introduced the two men. They shook hands, although Wyatt looked as if he'd rather arm wrestle.

Is he jealous?

Jealously suggested he had deeper feelings. And although she figured he was attracted to her, to imagine it was anything more than that would be foolish.

Once Cameron left to start his rotation on the

beach, Wyatt leaned against the counter and crossed his arms. "Old boyfriend?"

Fiona folded her roster into her pocket. "Old friend," she said and offered to show Wyatt around. "The whole top floor is being refurbished after a fire a few months ago," she explained as she motioned for them to head from the office and into one of the three larger rooms out front. "The local residents' committee worked hard to get the funding and the project will take about eight months to finish. The space upstairs is used for courses in self-defense and martial-arts classes. And downstairs for things like first-aid skills training."

"Fiona?"

She walked toward the stairway. "Of course, it's wonderful to have a newly refurbished building for people to come and—"

"Fiona, stop."

She stilled as her foot hit the bottom stair.

"I want to talk to you about what Cecily said."

Fiona didn't feel like dealing with that particular issue. She'd talk with her daughter privately about how they were *not* holding hands. With-out Wyatt around to distract her. "I'd rather not."

He didn't let up. "She's just being *Cecily.*"

"She thought we were holding hands," Fiona said as awkwardness crept along her skin.

"Actually, we *were* holding hands. But that's not the point. You don't have to worry. She's fine with it."

"I don't want her to be fine with it," she re-plied sharply. "Or her to think I'm…that I'm…"

"That you're what?"

"Easy," she breathed out.

Wyatt took a step toward her. "Easy?" he echoed. "Because I was holding your hand?"

Fiona dropped her shoulders. "Because I was… Because we were…" She stopped and filled her lungs with air. "Maybe it doesn't make sense to you, but I don't want her to think I would do anything to act on…" She waved a hand be-tween them. "*This.* We kissed and that compli-cates things."

"If we let it."

"Sure, if we let it. Only, I'm not the kind of

person who gets involved casually. I want Cecily to know I'm someone who makes good choices. Let's face it, I'm at a disadvantage. I've got a lot of ground to make up."

Fiona meant every word. It was important she behaved like a woman her daughter could respect. Lusting after Wyatt didn't put her in that category.

"Cecily is a good judge of character," he said and took a couple of steps upward. "She'll make up her mind about you because of what she knows about you now and not because of something you did when you were fifteen years old. The only person who believes you are defined by that moment, Fiona, is you." He kept walking and reached the landing.

"But the investigator's report—"

"Was a stupid idea," he said and cut her off. "And you were right—it was a piece of paper. It didn't tell me who you were. It didn't tell me that you were honest and kind and clearly a good person. I know you'll do what's right for Cecily."

Fiona's breath caught in her throat. "Thank

you," she said and knew she sounded wobbly. "That means a lot."

He nodded. "So, let's get on with this tour you promised me."

She got her attention back on track and climbed the stairs. There was a class in progress on one side of room, which was sectioned off from the remaining space with trestles and painting gear left from the workers who'd been in the building the day before. A small group of elderly women were doing tai chi, and they watched the participants through the glass door.

"This will be a great facility when it's complete. The funding was a lifeline for the building."

"You're frowning," he observed.

"Am I?" She shrugged lightly. "I was thinking how I wished we could get the same windfall for the school where I work."

"You want a place where the kids can practice tai chi?"

She smiled as his lame joke. "We need a new canteen."

"Something wrong with the old one?" he asked and followed as she headed back down the stairs.

"Everything," she replied. "We've applied for funding every year for the last…" She paused and did a mental calculation. "Well, the five years I've been teaching there and another two years before that."

"I gather it's not a high priority."

"Not exactly," she said unhappily. "It has a roof and four walls—apparently that's all the kids need. Mostly it needs renovating—you know, new walls inside, some painting, that sort of thing."

"Have you tried fundraising?"

"For sure," she said as they walked through the front door and back onto the pathway, avoiding a pair of wobbly cyclists. "And we've had some success. But people's purses only stretch so far, and in between saving the foreshore, the seabirds, the mangroves and the local turtle population, there's not a lot left over for one tiny school and its need for a new canteen."

150 · HIS-AND-HERS FAMILY

"Kids should have a place to buy food, though." He stopped walking. "Show me."

"Show you? Why?"

"I'm curious. Can you access school grounds on the weekend?"

Fiona nodded. "Of course. It's school break so it won't make any difference. But I don't understand why—"

"Like I said, I'm curious."

She didn't understand his motives but didn't see the harm. "Okay. How about tomorrow? I'll clear it with the principal to make sure. About nine o'clock."

"It's a date," Wyatt said easily and headed for the sand hills and disappeared over the embankment.

Wyatt picked her up the following morning at three minutes to nine o'clock. Alone. Fiona hopped into his rental car and tried not the think about how her heart was doing a kind of silly fluttering thing as she gave quick directions to the school.

"Where's Cecily?" she asked as she put on her seat belt.

Wyatt slanted her a sideways look. "With Trevor. I'm learning to trust. Impressed?"

"I don't imagine it's something you do easily."

"Trust?" He steered the car around. "Probably not."

She dropped her small tote at her feet. "I suppose it's natural to be wary after you've been, you know…"

"Cheated on?"

Fiona nodded. "Did you suspect it? I mean, before—"

"Before I caught her in bed with someone else? No."

She didn't bother to hide her distaste. Perhaps it was a leftover hang-up from all the years she spent on the road with Shayne, watching her mother fall into the arms of one cowboy after another, many of them married men with families. It was a behavior she'd vowed to never emulate. And then Jamie Corbett came along and took what she wasn't prepared to give.

"We're not all like that," she said and quickly realized how intimate it sounded.

"I know," he replied lightly. "It takes two people to cheat."

"Monogamy doesn't seem like much of a price if you really love someone."

He looked at her. "*If* you love someone? Exactly. I'll probably thank Yvette one day."

Yvette? It was a fancy-sounding name. Fiona would bet her frayed sneakers that his ex-fiancée was beautiful. She suddenly wished she'd done something stupidly female like slap on a little makeup that morning. Or at least deck herself out in new jeans instead of the old favorites that fit like a glove but were older than Methuselah.

"Do you still see her?"

Sheesh...isn't that the dumbest, most painfully obvious question ever uttered?

Thankfully they pulled up in front of the school before Fiona had to decide if he was grinning. She opened the door as swiftly as she could and grabbed her bag.

"The gate is over—"

Wyatt looked at her over the top of the vehicle. "I don't see Yvette," he said. "I'm not seeing anyone. Just so you know."

"I do know," she said quickly and shut the door. "Cecily told me. I mean, I'm sure there are many women who would want to go out with you." Fiona stopped and cringed as heat crept over her skin and up her neck. "I only meant that if you were seeing someone you wouldn't have…you know…"

"Kissed you?" He was grinning.

She ignored his words and waved an arm toward the school. "We're here."

"Let's take a look."

Fifteen minutes later, Wyatt stepped back from the doorway leading into the canteen area and looked up toward the roof.

"Well, it needs rebuilding, that's for sure."

Fiona's hopes sank. "Really? Which means thousands of dollars, right?"

"Tens of thousands."

Her eyes popped wide. "But it looks almost structurally sound."

"Termites," he explained. "Which have compromised the building's structural integrity. It needs to be pulled down. No decent builder would attempt renovation."

Fiona sank onto one of the low lunch seats underneath a shelter. Designed for the first graders, the position forced her knees up almost to her chin. "Well, that's that, then."

Wyatt swiveled on his heels. "Not necessarily."

She looked up. "Without funding, we couldn't possibly afford to rebuild."

He stepped back and shrugged in a way that made her stare at his shoulders and think how well he pulled off the whole jeans-and-white-T-shirt thing. "You could with some help."

"Yeah, but as I said yesterday, there are so many different causes and our school—"

"I'll help you," he said, cutting her off.

Fiona jumped to her feet. "Why would you want to do that?"

He looked toward the building for a moment. "Because you… Because the school needs a new building. And because I'd like to."

"Wyatt, I couldn't possibly let you—"

"You talk with whoever you need to and I'll get plans drawn up. Harper's has a charity fund, and helping places like your school is exactly what the fund is for. My company will supply all the materials, and from this end you can work your magic and organize the contract labor."

"My magic?" she echoed, feeling more than a little spun out by his suggestion.

"Yeah," he said and smiled. "I'm sure you'll be able to coax a few volunteers."

Fiona planted her hands on her hips. "Why are you doing this?"

"Because the kids need a canteen," he replied. "And I need something to do for the next two weeks."

Was he so bored? It miffed her a bit. This was her home. Did he find the place so lacking? *Does he find me lacking?* Of course he did. She'd never been able to hold any man's attention. Why would Wyatt be any different? *Not that I actually want his attention.*

"Sure," she replied, not one to pass up such

an offer. The school did need a new building. Refusing help would be foolish. "I'll have to speak with Annette Brewer, the principal. But I'm certain she'll be only too happy to accept your generosity."

"Good. Once we get started with plans and submit for council approval, I reckon it will be about four months and you'll have a new canteen for your kids."

Fiona drew in some air. "Thank you, Wyatt. We should get going," she suggested, pushing back her budding irritation because he might be bored with her, and her growing attraction for him. "By the way, I promised Cecily I'd take her shopping tomorrow for our Christmas-in-July celebration."

They walked past the administration block in step with one another.

"No socks."

She snapped her head sideways. "Socks?"

"From Cecily," he replied. "No socks, ties or, heaven forbid, handkerchiefs."

Fiona laughed and it urged her a little away

from her bad mood. "The perfect gift for the man who has everything."

"Not everything," he corrected.

They were at the car and she allowed him to open her door. "Is there anything you'd like?" she asked and felt the heat rise up between them the moment the words left her mouth.

Wyatt moved closer, and Fiona pushed back against the door. "Anything?"

"Yes. To ease your boredom maybe?"

"My what?"

"Isn't that why you want to help out here?" she asked. "Because you're bored?"

He reached across and looped a lock of her hair between his fingers. "Ah, Fiona, you know, you're killing me," he said softly and touched her cheek. "I'm not bored…I'm frustrated as hell."

"Sorry." Fiona shuddered out a breath. His fingertips, warm against her skin, curved over her jaw and cupped her chin.

"Me, too." His thumb traced her bottom lip. "Sorry, I can't stop thinking about kissing you again. Or stop imagining what it would be like to—"

A car passed and beeped loudly. Fiona recognized Cameron's police patrol vehicle immediately and ducked sideways. "Please," she said as the car traveled up the road. "Someone could see and I…" She stopped and straightened. "Please, take me back."

He pulled back instantly. "Of course."

When they were both in the car, Fiona summoned the gumption to say what was on her mind. There was no point in putting it off. It had to be said. "Wyatt, I can't be alone with you like this," she admitted and felt her heart tighten. It *was* right to say. But it hurt. It hurt so much. "I'm not going to get involved with you any more than I already am. It's blurring… the reason you're here—and Cecily. I have to stay focused. I won't make this situation about myself. I have a chance to get back something I thought I'd lost, and I don't want to risk that. Not for anything."

Not even for you.

He took a moment, then spoke. "It won't happen again."

"That's what we said yesterday," she said on a sigh. "You know, I've been alone most of my life. Even when I lived with my uncle, I was alone. He tried, but most days I felt as though I lived in this singular vacuum, apart from everyone and everything. And now…" She paused, eyes down, head bent. "Now, for the first time in a long time, I don't feel alone. And I'm not sure if it's because of Cecily…or because of you."

"Fiona, I—"

"Let me finish, please," she protested and raised her hands before dropping them back into her lap. "There's no point in whitewashing this. The truth is, I don't want to find that at the end of these few weeks I have a whole lot of…feelings. I don't want to fall for you. I don't want to fall for anyone. I just want a chance to be what Cecily needs me to be. I love my daughter," she said. "And she's all I have space inside myself for."

She noticed he gripped the steering wheel. "I'll take you back."

As he started the ignition and eased the car onto the road, she knew she'd made her point. In two and a half weeks, he'd be gone. After that, she figured Cecily would commute during holidays to visit. He wouldn't have to return to Crystal Point again.

The realization didn't settle the discontent in her heart. Or the knowledge she was in deep. Way deep.

"So, he's building the school canteen himself?"

Fiona sat lotus-style on her sofa and nodded to her friend. Callie dipped a spoon into a tub of vanilla ice cream topped with chocolate sauce and Oreo cookies and looked at her after she'd asked the question.

"His company is supplying the funds for plans and materials," Fiona replied. "We're organizing the labor from this end."

"And he's doing this because…?" M.J. asked

as she grabbed a spoon and dug into her own tub of chocolate-mint.

Fiona shrugged and ignored the way her stomach rolled. Thinking about Wyatt had been off her agenda for two days. She wasn't about to put him back on it. "To help the school."

"Or to get into your good books?" Callie suggested with raised brows.

"Or your pants?" M.J. offered with a delightful squeal.

Callie tossed a cushion at her sister-in-law. "Behave," she admonished playfully.

Fiona did her best impression of a poker face. "He wants something to do, that's all. I suspect he's bored since Cecily and I are together most days."

"I like the whole panty concept better," M.J. said and scooped a mouthful of ice cream. "Much more exciting."

"Will you let up?" Evie scolded her sister and dipped an Oreo into ice-cold milk.

M.J. smiled and raised her provocative brows. "Although, if you are going to toss your panties, who better than that gorgeous man to catch them?"

It was Friday night and her friends had abandoned their pottery class at Evie's studio for an evening at Fiona's. Cecily, Lily and another friend were in the guest bedroom playing Wii karaoke and shoving down copious amount of soda, potato chips and cold pizza.

"I think it's admirable that he wants to help. So, instead of questioning his motives, accept it as an act of goodwill," Evie said. She appeared to be the only one not romanticizing the whole situation. And Fiona needed an ally tonight.

"Exactly," Fiona managed to squeak out, still reeling from the whole tossed-panties idea.

"He's taken over my office," Evie said as she dipped another cookie. "Not that I mind, of course, if it means the school will benefit. But he doesn't talk much. Seems like a man with a lot on his mind."

Fiona offered a smile, which didn't quite cut the mark, and Callie pushed herself off the sofa.

"Let's go and make some more tea," her friend suggested.

She nodded and followed her friend down the hallway. Once they reached the kitchen, Callie turned. "Do you like him?" she asked.

Fiona stepped back. "Like him? If you mean—"

"You know exactly who I mean. And what I mean."

She didn't bother to deny it. "Sure. I like him."

"And he likes you, right?"

"I guess."

Callie's blue eyes widened. "But you're avoiding him?"

She shrugged. "We're keeping it real."

"What does that mean?"

"The situation," Fiona replied. "Why he's here. Why Cecily's here. I want to have a relationship with my daughter."

"Who says you can't have both?"

"I say." She grabbed hold of the counter. "I never get the guy, Callie. I always get the let's-be-friends speech at the end of it. And when it's done and dusted, I never speak with them again because I'm so humiliated. I don't want that to happen here. I won't let it. Do I like him? Yes. Do I want him? Yes. But I won't get wrapped up in some romantic notion...not when there's so much at stake."

"Cecily?"

She nodded. "Loving a child...it's life-altering."

"Yes," Callie said and watched her. "But so is loving a man."

She didn't know that. Her few and brief relationships had been infatuations, nothing more. And when over they'd left her what? Not heartbroken. Not anything really. It kept her safe, whole. Becoming unhinged, being *all* feelings. She thought she wanted it, but now, when looking directly into the face of those kinds of feelings, Fiona was terrified.

She drew in a breath, grappling for a strength she didn't quite feel. "I am not going to fall in love with Wyatt Harper."

I'm not...

* * *

On Saturday morning, Wyatt opened his emails and took a call from Glynis, who worked through his request to incorporate the Crystal Point School as a recipient of the Harper charity fund. He also emailed his sister Ellen, who was on the board, and asked her to push the request through quickly. Once the correct paperwork was filed and the board in agreement, he could take steps to submit the building plans through council. He'd forgotten how much he liked creating plans. Since being drafted into Harper's only two years after graduating from college, he hadn't had much use for his architecture degree. His father's second heart attack had changed Wyatt's plan to work outside of the family business for a few years before taking over the reins of the company.

But drawing up the plans for the small school building was satisfying and it shifted his mind off other things.

Fiona...

He hadn't seen her for three days, although he

got daily updates from Cecily about their activities—from shopping to horse riding to a girls' night in with a group of friends. His niece was happier than she'd been for a long time. Maybe ever.

It was strange how that realization didn't bring up a whole lot of loyalty issues. He was usually fiercely protective of his family. But his loyalties were conflicted. He liked Fiona. And his attraction for her had grown from a slow-burning awareness to a fierce need.

And she wasn't giving him the time of day.

It stung. Even though he understood her motives. She was right. Getting involved was out of the question. But logic, once a strong ally in his organized life, had deserted him. He didn't feel the least bit logical when it came to Fiona. Because his desire for her, which a week ago, he was convinced, had been about physical attraction and sex, had somehow morphed into something else. Something deeper.

He liked her. And he...missed her.

Idiot.

She was messing with his head. He *never* got this way. Not even Yvette had distracted him so much. Why was that? Why did someone he'd known mere weeks twist his insides like a pretzel? And why the hell was she ignoring him? Okay, so she didn't want to get involved. He didn't, either, did he?

Except all he could think about was seeing her again.

Chapter Seven

"So, how come you don't have a boyfriend?"

Fiona was in the kitchen making lasagna for her daughter's sleepover at Lily's house when Cecily popped her head into the room with Muffin in her arms and asked the question.

"What?"

"A boyfriend?" her daughter asked, moving into the room. "It's just that you're really pretty and a nice person—you *should* have a boyfriend."

Fiona placed the cheese grater on the countertop. Talks about boyfriends were part of being a parent but she wasn't exactly prepared for them. Plus, she'd imagined the talk would be about her daughter's dating life, not her own. "It's not that simple. I haven't met anyone I liked for a while."

Cecily looked at her and smiled. "Do you like Uncle Wyatt?"

The million-dollar question. And one she should have expected. "Well, I—"

"I mean, I know you like him," Cecily said, cutting her off as she placed Muffin on the floor. "But do you *like* him?"

Fiona sucked in a breath, fought back her embarrassment and faced her daughter. "Where's this all coming from?"

Cecily shrugged again, less enthusiastic this time, and pulled out a chair. When she slumped into it, Fiona knew her daughter had something big on her mind. In the brief time she'd known Cecily, Fiona had been in awe of her happy-go-lucky personality and constant smiles. But in the past couple of days, as their relationship had developed, she'd observed something else. A mother's instinct perhaps. She wasn't sure. But there was something going on with her.

"I don't know," she said after a moment. She rested her elbows on the table and propped her chin in her palm. "I only thought it would be sort of nice if you guys liked each other in that way."

That way? The problem was Fiona did like Wyatt in *that* way. Very much. But anything happening between them was out of the question. She'd made her resolve very clear.

"We've become friends," she said carefully. "And we both agree that you are what's important at the moment."

Cecily's eyes widened and she gave a little smile. "So, if it's all about me, I should get what I want, right?"

Fiona stilled. "Er—that depends on what it is."

"I want what I used to have," she said and looked as though she were doing her best to sound cheerful. "Look, don't get me wrong, Nan and Pop are great and I love them a lot. But they're my *grandparents* and they're old. I know they are pretty cool for their age, but Pop's already had a couple of heart attacks and what if…what if they…die soon?"

Fiona's heart surged. "Is that what you're afraid will happen?"

"I guess." She nodded and let out a heavy sigh. "I know Uncle Wyatt is my legal guardian, and he tries to spend time with me when he can. But he's busy and has to run the company and can only get to Waradoon on the weekends. I just thought that if he got, you know, married or something, then it would be like it was when my parents were alive. Like a proper family."

Her words cut through Fiona like a blade. A proper family? How often had she longed for that when she was a child? Even now, in her deepest heart, the longing remained. And her daughter, who had endured so much loss in her short life, was now echoing her own secret wish.

"There are all kinds of families and each one is unique." She took the seat next to Cecily and grasped her hand. "Your grandparents love you. As does your uncle, and I'm sure your aunts feel the same. And I love you."

Cecily's bright blue-gray eyes glittered. "I know. I'm grateful for everyone caring about me, really I am. But having a mother and father and being together all the time…that's how it should be. Even when I knew my parents weren't happy together sometimes, at least we were together. Being together is what's important."

Fiona caught the tremor in Cecily's voice. It wasn't the first time her daughter had intimated that Jim and Karen Todd's relationship had been anything other than perfect. But all marriages went through challenging times, didn't they?

"They fought," Cecily said quietly, as though unsure if she should be saying anything about it. "Not always. I wasn't supposed to know. But I heard them sometimes. I'd hear my mother crying and Dad kept saying he was sorry all the time. And then it sort of got better. Except then they died."

Fiona squeezed her hand. "It's normal to want things that make you feel safe."

"I guess. I just don't want Uncle Wyatt to marry someone I don't like," she said, sounding every one of her fourteen years. "Like what's-her-name."

Fiona was pretty sure Cecily knew exactly what the other woman's name was, and smiled to herself. "Well, unfortunately, I don't think you get a say in who he marries."

Neither do I.

"But if he married you, we'd be a real family."

Marry Wyatt? Sweet heaven. Despite the crazy fluttering in her belly, Fiona knew she had to put a halt to Cecily's active imagination. "We're not getting married. We're not in love. And that's the only reason why two people should get married."

It sounded good. It sounded as if she meant every word. But in her head it sounded too good. *I'm trying too hard here.*

"So, let's get the lasagna cooked for this sleepover and I'll drop you at Lily's."

Cecily smiled. "Sure. And thanks, Fiona—thanks for listening."

"Anytime," she said and hugged her as they stood.

Maybe I'll get this mothering thing right after all.

* * *

Wyatt pulled the car outside Fiona's at precisely three minutes to seven. He'd had five hours to figure out what he was doing and came up with zilch.

I shouldn't be here.

Too late to back out now, he thought as he walked up the driveway. He heard her little dog bark. The door opened before he made it to the bottom step.

She looked beautiful.

So lovely he could hardly draw breath, which seemed to have become an all-too-frequent reaction when he was within six feet of her. She wore a long white skirt and soft green sweater scooped out wide over her shoulders. The awareness quickly turned into an all-out surge of raw hunger so fierce he could barely swallow.

Great start.

"Wyatt?"

"Hi," he said and took the steps. "Did Cecily get to her party okay?"

"Yes. What's that?"

He held up the wine bottle in his hand. "From a local winery a short stretch from Waradoon."

She looked at him and frowned. "What are you doing here?"

"I thought…I thought we could talk."

"Talk?"

She looked about as convinced of that as he did. "Yeah. I haven't seen you for a while and figured we needed to touch base about Cecily."

Her eyes widened. "Is something wrong? Have I done something to—"

"Nothing's wrong," he assured her. "I just wanted to talk."

Her expression went from concern to suspicion. "At night, alone and with a bottle of wine?" One brow came up. "Do you really think that's a good idea?"

"Probably not." He let out a heavy breath. She didn't want him on her doorstep. He should have had more sense. "You're right. I'll go."

"It's okay," she said quickly and moved back through the door. "You're here now, so you may as well come inside."

"Are you sure?"

She nodded and Wyatt followed her through the door. He was immediately drawn into the unique warmth of her little house. The textured shabby-chic furniture, paisley throws and craftwork dotted around the living room were far removed from the contemporary lines of his city apartment or the country charm of Waradoon. But something about the place had an unusual calming effect.

The dog shuffled around his feet for a moment and then scurried into her wicker basket in the corner of the room.

"I'll get glasses."

She disappeared down the hall and Wyatt let out a breath. *Keep your head.* He cruised around the room for a moment and lingered by a cabinet along one wall. There were photographs in frames—of her horse and her friends. He searched for anyone who looked like family. It made him think of the big staircase at Waradoon and the gallery of photographs lining the walls that displayed generations of Harpers.

"I'd like to get one of Cecily."

She was behind him, holding glasses and a corkscrew. "Of course," he said and took the items from her. "I can take some of you together if you like?"

"Yes, I would like that."

"Is that your mother?" he asked when he spotted a faded picture stuck into the corner of a larger frame.

She stepped closer. "Yes. That's Shayne."

"Shayne?"

"She liked me to call her by her first name. It made it easier for her."

"Easier to what?" he asked and opened the wine.

Fiona stared at the photograph for a moment. "To pick up," she said as she turned away and sat on an overstuffed love seat in the corner. "Didn't you get that about her from your investigation?" she asked and held out the glasses.

"I was more interested in you." *And still am.*

After a moment, Fiona spoke. "She was a buckle bunny."

Wyatt stilled. "A what?"

She said it again. "A woman who follows the rodeo circuit," she explained. "Not a pretty story."

Wyatt half filled their glasses and sat on the sofa. Miles away from her. Although he felt the vibration coming off her skin. "And a hard one to tell?"

She shrugged. "I guess, like all sad childhood stories. Shayne was kind of lost. Unfortunately she dragged me through her lost world for many years."

"Before you went to live with your uncle?"

"When I was expecting Cecily."

"And your mother died a few weeks later."

"Yes, in a railway-crossing accident. She was an addict anyway…which probably would have killed her if the train hadn't."

Wyatt didn't bother to hide his surprise.

"Does that sound harsh?" she asked and sipped her wine. "Maybe it does. She was my mother, but I was rarely *mothered,* if that makes sense. She drank a lot, used drugs when she could get her hands on them, drifted from one place to the next looking for someone…some man to hold on to. I felt alone most of the time."

He stretched back into the seat and rested the wineglass on the arm. "And Cecily's father?"

Shutters came up. "I don't want to talk about that."

"You'll have to at some point."

"Why?" she queried. "It's in the past. You said I wasn't defined by my past."

"I know what I said. I meant because Cecily will want to know."

She drew in a heavy breath. "I just don't want to dredge up a whole lot of painful stuff that really—"

"Painful?" he echoed quietly and looked directly into her eyes. "What happened to you, Fiona? You're trying so hard to not talk about it."

Her eyes were bright. "What I'm *trying* to do is look to the future and not dwell on the past. I want to concentrate on this short amount of time I have with Cecily. But if you're concerned about the way I'm handling things with her, I would—"

"Actually, for someone who had an emotionally absent mother, you're quite remarkable with Cecily." Wyatt propped his glass on a side table. "In fact, I've never seen her happier. I'm not about to pull her out from under you, Fiona. So relax."

"Relax? Around you?" She gave a brittle laugh. "You can't be serious. I've never been less relaxed in my life."

Wyatt shrugged. "If it's any consolation, I feel the same way."

"Then why are you here?" she asked.

"Because I wanted to see you. Without Cecily. Without Evie. Without any one of your numerous friends standing guard."

Wyatt got to his feet and stared out the window. She wished she knew what he was thinking. His broad shoulders looked tense and she fought the urge to go to him. It was better this way. Better to stay strong.

"We agreed we wouldn't do anything."

He turned back toward her. "I know that. Which doesn't mean I have to like it."

Fiona swallowed hard. She didn't like it, either. But wasn't about to admit that. She needed to stay grounded and keep her head. Her relationship with Cecily depended on it.

"You know, we've been thrown together because of the situation with Cecily. I'm not so naive that I'd think for one minute you'd be interested in me in other circumstances."

Annoyance sharpened his expression. "You think I'm attracted to you because it's convenient?"

"Well, I—"

"Believe me, Fiona, for the past few days it has felt damned inconvenient."

Fiona shot up from her seat and wobbled on her heels. "Well, it hasn't exactly been a picnic for me, either!"

The room filled with heat, swirling around, catching her skin, her blood and her quaking bones. It took about three seconds to register Wyatt's expression as it changed from irritation to raw desire. There was no denying it. And Fiona couldn't deny it, either. She wanted him. It was clear he wanted her, too.

"Cecily wants you to get married," she said, trying to grasp on to some sense, some way of holding off the feelings running riot through her body, and hoping it would have the effect of a bucket of cold water over the rising desire whirling between them.

He raised a brow. "To whom?"

"To someone she likes. She wants parents again—a mother and a father."

"I suppose that's to be expected." He moved across the room. "She had that before. It makes sense she'd want it again."

Fiona stepped back and her legs collided with the love seat. "She said…she said something today. She said your sister and her husband weren't completely happy."

He looked at her sharply for a second and then shrugged. "They had some problems."

"What kind of problems?"

Wyatt moved around the coffee table and grabbed her hand. "What does it matter?"

"Cecily said—"

"It was nothing," he said and threaded their fingers. "Enough about them."

He pulled her toward him and she went without protest. Some faraway voice told her to resist, but the echo quickly faded as he drew her against him. "Wyatt, I—"

"And enough talk," he said gently. "I'd rather kiss you."

"We said we wouldn't."

"Yeah…but that promise isn't working out so well for me. Is it for you?"

Fiona shook her head. "Not so far."

"If you want me to go, I'll go. If you want me to stop, I'll stop."

She moved against him and curved an arm up to his shoulder. "I don't want you to go," she breathed. "And I don't want you to stop."

He smiled, dipped his head and captured her lips. Fiona opened her mouth and gave herself up to his possession. Heat fueled her blood, and she grasped his shoulders to steady her weakening limbs. Wyatt's kiss was soft and seductive, and as he slanted his mouth over hers, she leaned into his embrace. Every ounce of longing in her heart rose up, and she knew, without a doubt, that what she was feeling was more than just desire. All her plans not to fall for Wyatt deserted her the moment he groaned against her lips and whispered how much he wanted her.

They didn't make it to her bedroom. She urged him backward to the sofa, still kissing, still feeling and wanting like she'd never wanted before. The tiny voice in the back of her mind telling her to stop before things went too far became a distant echo. Recriminations could come later. The moment was now. And for once, she longed to live in the moment.

He laid her gently on the big sofa, knelt beside her and kissed her again. When he trailed his mouth from her lips to the incredibly sensitive spot below her ear, Fiona shuddered. She grasped his shoulders and felt the heat of his mouth against her collarbone and moaned when his tongue trailed across her skin. He pushed the sweater off her shoulder and kissed her there, and then down toward the rise of her breast. His hand splayed over her rib cage and beneath the sweater, and he drew tiny circles with his fingertips. Fiona sighed with pleasure and moved her hands over his shoulders and down his arms. His biceps were solid, strong, and suddenly it occurred to her that everything about Wyatt was strong. His character, his integrity, his very self. *That's why I'm falling.* It wasn't only that his touch made her come alive. Without knowing how, Fiona's feelings surged from physical desire to a raw emotional need.

She tugged at his shirt and he quickly chucked it over his head. His chest was so well cut Fiona swallowed hard before she traced her hands over the defined muscles. He trembled when she touched him, and her growing feelings rose to the surface. She might have blurted it out had he not possessed her lips in a searing, drugging kiss.

His hands were suddenly impatient and he

pushed her sweater up. The filmy bra she wore did little to hide her pebbled nipples, and when his mouth closed over one, she arched her back. Pleasure arrowed downward in a rush and she gripped his hips, looping her fingers around the band of his jeans. She was all impatience, all need, all want. Wyatt smiled as he kissed her. It didn't take long for him to ease her sweater off and flick the two hooks holding her bra. Topless, Fiona fought the urge to cover herself. But there was no need for coyness. Wyatt clearly liked what he saw and touched her breasts again, caressing her with skillful seduction. Her nipples ached for him and he gently flicked one tight bud with his tongue while he pushed her skirt over her hips. Within seconds the garment was on the floor. Her briefs quickly followed.

Naked beneath his penetrating gaze, Fiona forgot her usual insecurities. A man didn't fake that kind of desire. The freckles felt like sun kisses; the faded stretch marks on her belly from when her teenage body had carried a child didn't fill her with the usual modesty. Wyatt knew her story. He knew her.

"You're so lovely," he said as he stood and kicked off his shoes. Jeans and boxer briefs followed.

Mesmerized by the sheer magnitude of his beauty and arousal, Fiona pressed back against the sofa and raised her arms in clear invitation. He took a second to extract something from his jeans, and she squashed a frown back when he placed a condom on the table. The idea that he'd prepared for this and that he might have expected it created a little resentment, a little uncertainty. But then she remembered how much she wanted him, despite her feeble denials over the previous week, and all her doubts were forgotten.

He lay beside her, and Fiona was eternally grateful she had a big couch. She'd never sit on it again without remembering how it felt to have Wyatt pressed intimately against her. He kissed her hotly and she returned each kiss, savoring the taste of him and the feel of his tongue wrapped around hers. Fiona couldn't get enough of him. His skin, like silk stretched over hot steel, was divine beneath her fingertips. He touched her breasts, her hips, her belly and lower to where she screamed to be touched. His fingers worked magic, sending her wild and quickly to the brink. When she could take no more, when she felt herself falling, Fiona found her voice.

"Wyatt…now…please."

He didn't stop. "Not yet," he whispered against her mouth. "I want you to come apart."

"But you—"

He silenced her with a kiss and touched her with gentle intimacy, touched her like no other man ever had. As if he knew, somehow, what she longed for, what she needed. The pressure built, taking her higher, making her fly. When her body exploded in a burst of incandescent pleasure, he held her through it, kissing her, stroking her over and over as the pulsing waves receded and she returned to earth.

When she could breathe again, Fiona looked into his eyes and with a tiny smile reached out a hand and grabbed the condom. She'd never been the seductive type. Her lingering hang-ups about what happened when she was fifteen whirled around her head for a moment. She'd taken sex back a long time ago, refusing to allow one person's brutality to hold her hostage for the rest of her life. But being with Wyatt made her realize she had been holding back. Waiting for this. Waiting for him. As she ripped the foil packet with her teeth and watched his expression darken with desire, Fiona felt sexier than she ever had in her life.

He grinned and took the condom. Seconds later he moved over her. Fiona gripped his shoulders and didn't waver from his gaze as he entered her slowly. There was nothing hasty about Wyatt. He took his time, watching her as she shifted her body to accommodate him inside her in the most intimate way possible. It felt right. It felt real. When he moved, stars exploded behind her eyes and she held on tight, feeling more a part of him than she ever had of anyone.

"Wyatt...I..."

"I know," he said against her lips as they moved together. "I know."

It was like another world, a world she'd only ever dreamed of. A world where she was desired so completely, so profoundly, nothing but wanting and pleasure and raw hunger existed. And she was in that world, driven by longing, by the relentless need to feel him everywhere and in every way imaginable. His skin, his kiss, his breath…everything reached her, everything made her want him more.

The tension built, the rhythm became a mutual ride as they moved together, as one, joined by more than bodies. Fiona experienced pleasure so incredibly acute she shook with emotion as she climaxed. When he followed moments later, she held on, giving, taking and holding him with all that lay in her heart as he shuddered against her.

When their breathing returned to something resembling normal, and still taking all his weight on his elbows, Wyatt looked down into her face.

"Are you all right?"

She managed to nod and whispered, "Yes."

"Regrets?"

"Right now?" She smiled and touched his face. "No. Later…probably."

He drew in a heavy breath. "Well, that's honest at least. I think you're probably the most sincere woman I've ever met."

It was a lovely compliment, and because her emotions were jumping all over the place, she couldn't help the tears that filled her eyes. "Thank you."

He smiled gently and drew away from her. "Let's go to bed."

"Bed?" She shifted on the sofa, suddenly conscious of her nakedness and Wyatt's unmistakably semi-aroused state. "Oh, I thought…"

He stood up, reached for her hand and urged her to her feet. "You thought what? That we were done?" He gave a sexy laugh and pulled her close. "Oh, no, we're not done."

Fiona smiled and her heart rolled over. And she knew, at that moment, that she was completely and irrevocably in love with Wyatt Harper.

Chapter Eight

Morning-afters were never easy. And Fiona wasn't looking forward to this one.

She'd left Wyatt asleep in her bed. They'd made love again at dawn, and he'd wrung every ounce of pleasure from her. Physically spent, she'd dozed for an hour and woke when Muffin jumped up on her side of the bed. Wyatt hadn't stirred. She'd slipped out of bed, pushed her arms through a soft oversize T-shirt and lingered in the doorway for a moment. He slept on his stomach, one arm outstretched, and his dark hair was a stark contrast against the white pillow. She was tempted to crawl back into bed and trace her fingers up and down his smooth skin.

Instead she took a quick shower and then padded down the hall into the kitchen, fed the dog and cranked up the coffee machine.

Well, I've gone and done it now.

She pressed her hips against the countertop and let out a heavy breath. Okay, so they'd had sex. And she'd realized she was in love with him. But in the cold light of morning, clarity returned. Loving him was one thing…but imagining he loved her in return was something else altogether. Love hadn't rated a mention during the past twelve hours. She certainly wasn't about to announce her newly realized feelings.

Fiona poured herself a cup of coffee, took a long drink and waited for the caffeine to kick in.

It didn't help much. With Wyatt asleep down the hall, her body aching in places she'd forgotten could ache and her mind reeling with the knowledge she had fallen in love with a man she hardly knew, Fiona needed more than a double espresso to calm her nerves.

She pushed the coffee aside and sat down.

So, think. Think hard. And think quickly. Because he's not going to stay asleep forever. And I'll have to talk to him.

But think what? That it was a onetime thing? A quick roll in the hay? Physical attraction gone wild. A one-night stand?

Ouch.

Fiona didn't do one-nighters. Ever. She'd seen firsthand the damage indiscriminate sex could cause. Shayne's example was burned into her memory bank. Her head felt as if it would explode when she considered the enormity of what she'd done. *Some good example I am for my daughter.*

She didn't want Cecily to think she was… what? A flake like Shayne? She'd told Wyatt she didn't want her daughter to think she was easy. But it was more than that. She'd missed out on fourteen years. Years where Cecily had managed quite effectively without her. Years where she'd had near-perfect parents. And a perfect mother.

She couldn't compete with that. She didn't

want to be Karen Todd. She could only be herself. More importantly, a version of herself whom Cecily could respect. Fiona had to show her daughter she was reliable, dependable...worthy.

And a one-night stand with Wyatt didn't make her fit into that category.

Despite Cecily's eagerness to get them together, Fiona knew it was a fantasy. He'd be gone in two weeks and Cecily would be gone with him. Of course, she'd still see her daughter during school breaks. But for Wyatt...it would be a holiday fling at best. Casual, noncommitted sex between two people attracted to one another. In other circumstances she might have been okay with that. She might have accepted whatever she could have of Wyatt even if only for a short time. But not with Cecily stuck in the middle.

When she heard the shower hiss a few moments later, she got to her feet, pulled out the makings of breakfast from the refrigerator and grabbed a fresh mug. Ten minutes later Wyatt walked into the kitchen. Jeans unbuttoned at the fly, bare chest, bare feet, hair damp and a towel tossed over one shoulder—he looked so good her knees wobbled.

"Coffee?" she asked as she grabbed a skillet from its hanging spot above the stove top.

"Sure," he said as he came to the other side of the bench. He rubbed a hand over his chin. "I need to shave."

Fiona barely dared to look at him. The faint stubble across his jaw was too sexy for words. And she remembered how the gentle abrasion had felt across her skin as he'd trailed kisses over every inch of her body. Too good.

"Are you hungry?" she asked as she pushed a mug across the bench.

He looked her over and grinned. "I guess we did forget to eat last night."

"I'll make breakfast now," she said so cheerfully her ears hurt.

Wyatt took the coffee. "I swiped a towel. Hope you don't mind."

She smiled and wondered if her jaw would

stick in that position. "Fine. How do you like your eggs?"

"Fried, scrambled." He shrugged. "Whatever."

Scrambled like my brain. "Omelet it is," she said and began cracking eggs into a bowl.

"Can I help?" he asked.

She pointed to the cutlery draw. "You can set the table."

"Sure." He got the job done quickly and came back around to the counter. "You like to cook?"

"I guess," she replied. "I like to make cakes. Sometimes I make them and take them over to Callie's. The kids always go crazy for my fudge brownies."

"I'm sure they do."

Oh, Lord, it sounded so sickly sweet, and if they were any more excruciatingly polite, Fiona's teeth would fall out. "Actually, my baking's not the best, but the kids don't seem to care."

Fiona could feel the heat of his gaze on her. The thin cotton T-shirt seemed way more pro-vocative in the cold light of day—especially considering she wore nothing underneath. She remembered her discarded bra and briefs still on the floor in the living room and wished she'd shown the sense to snatch them up. Staring at his bare chest wasn't helping, either.

"Do you need help with anything else?"

She shook her head. "I'm good," she said and began whisking eggs.

He put his mug aside and braced his hands on the counter. "So, are we going to have the post-mortem now or after we eat?"

Fiona stopped whisking. "After," she said quietly and returned to the task. "Or not at all."

"We'll probably have to at some point."

She shrugged. "It is what it is."

"And what's that?"

Fiona felt his stare through to her bones. "You tell me… You're the one who came here with a condom in your pocket."

Wyatt rocked back on his heels. She sounded mad. Her cheeks were pink, her eyes as sharp as daggers. Okay, so she *was* mad. "Let me get this straight—you're angry because I brought protection?"

She dropped the utensil in her hand. "I'm not angry."

"No? So you just *look* like you want to whack me over the head with a frying pan?"

She glared at him, but he was relieved when he caught a little smile crinkling her lovely mouth. Of course, thinking about her mouth quickly crammed his head with memories of exactly what she'd done with it the night before. His libido spiked and wasn't helped one bit when she moved across the kitchen and the thin T-shirt, which only just reached her thighs, shimmied over her delightfully curvy bottom.

He cleared his throat and tried not to think about how much he wanted her again. They had to talk first. "Fiona?"

"I'm not angry," she said again. "I'm not anything. Honestly, I'm not exactly sure what I'm feeling at this point."

Wyatt appreciated her truth. "Look, I didn't come here last night just for..." He stopped himself from calling it *sex*. Because being with Fiona had felt way different from any sex he'd ever had before. "Let me try that again. I wanted to see you. Did I want to make love to you? Yes. Was that the only reason I was here? No. I like you, Fiona. That's why I'm here."

It sounded lukewarm at best, and Wyatt wasn't surprised that she looked as if she wished a great big hole would open up beneath his feet and swallow him.

But he wasn't about to admit to anything else. Or even consider anything else. He'd jumped quickly into his last relationship and it had ended in disaster. He'd met and proposed to Yvette within months. He wasn't about to do that again anytime soon. Whatever happened with Fiona, Wyatt knew now wasn't the time for any kind of declaration about feelings.

"What I'm trying to say is—"

"It's okay," she said, cutting him off as she banged the skillet. "I get it."

She looked so lovely with her hair curling around her face and her cheeks ablaze with color. Wyatt moved behind her. "Fiona, please turn around."

She stilled, dropped the skillet and turned. "Yes?"

Wyatt propped an arm on either side of her. "I'm not entirely sure what's going on in that beautiful head of yours."

She looked up and he noticed a pinkish mark on her neck. Not exactly a love bite, but close enough. The scent of her shampoo assailed his senses and kicked warmth through his blood. No one had ever had such a strong effect on his libido. She noticed the shifting mood and her blue-gray eyes shadowed with a sexy haze. Wyatt wrapped his arms around her and urged her close, then ran his hands down her hips and over her lovely behind. The moment he got a handful of bare skin and realized she was naked beneath the thin T-shirt, his building desire leaped forward like a racehorse at the starting gate.

When she dropped her forehead against his chest, he experienced a sharp and uncharacteristic pain behind his ribs. He kissed the top of her head, and she quickly shifted position and offered her lips to him. Wyatt took her mouth with such possessiveness he startled himself for a second. When he moved to pull back, Fiona pushed forward. She returned the kiss in the kind of hot, heady way he was becoming used to. She tugged at his fly and shoved his jeans down his hips, and he smiled at her eagerness. Need suddenly overshadowed finesse. He lifted her up and propped her on the edge of the bench.

"Fiona," he muttered against her lips. "Protection...we have to get—"

"Let's improvise," she suggested huskily and wrapped her legs around his waist.

Improvise? He could do that. Wyatt grabbed the towel dangling around his neck and tossed it on the counter behind her. "Okay," he breathed raggedly. He lifted her T-shirt and pushed it upward as he encouraged her to lie back. "Let's improvise."

She sighed as he ran his palm between her breasts and rib cage and lower, across her belly and lower still. She moaned her pleasure when he cupped her gently and parted the soft red hair covering her. She was divine. A goddess. *My woman,* he thought with an unusual pang of male possession. And he wanted to brand her with his kiss, his body, his very soul.

He kissed her belly, her hips, anointing every part of her with his mouth. And for the next hour they went beyond pleasure, beyond reason, beyond any feeling he'd experienced before.

Much later, once the passion had receded and they'd tumbled back into reality, they got dressed and then Wyatt finished cooking breakfast while Fiona fed the dog. They ate in silence, and he was painfully aware of the altering mood between them. Doubt and regret were suddenly filtering through the air, and by the time the meal was over, she seemed so wound up she looked as if she wanted to scream.

"I think…I think you should go."

Breakfast was over and the dishes done, and he stood by the countertop, watching her intently.

Her request wasn't a great surprise. "If that's what you want."

She nodded and moved around the table. "It is."

"Can I see you tonight?"

"No."

"Fiona, if we—"

"I don't want to see you," she said quickly and then added, "unless Cecily is with us."

He pushed down the stab of annoyance. "It's a bit late for a chaperone, don't you think?"

She sucked in a breath. "I told you I wanted to concentrate on Cecily, and despite what happened last night…and well, just before…despite all that, I still feel the same way. Cecily is what's important. This…" She waved a hand. "This is a complication neither of us need."

Wyatt looked deep into her eyes. She was right. He knew that. He'd brought Cecily to Crystal Point to meet her mother…not so he could get Fiona into bed. They'd crossed the line. Bigtime.

When he spoke again, there was quiet, deliberate control in his voice. "Then I'll see you Saturday…with Cecily. Goodbye, Fiona."

Fiona pulled the Christmas tree from its box and glanced at the impossible-to-comprehend instructions that came with it. She felt a little ridiculous putting up a tree in the middle of the year, but it was what Cecily wanted, and she was inclined to do whatever made her daughter happy. She really wasn't in any kind of mood to be assembling trees, but considering she'd promised Cecily, Fiona tried to develop some enthusiasm.

The fact her life was a mess had nothing to do with the fake tree and its incomprehensible instructions. She hadn't seen Wyatt for two days. Not since the morning where she'd completely lost her mind and did a whole lot of things with him that she'd never done with anyone ever before in her entire life.

Wild and erotic things. Things that made her cheeks burn with the memory. And her body burn with a shameless longing for more.

"I told you it was a cool tree," Cecily remarked

five minutes later once Fiona had plumped out the branches and plugged the transformer into the wall socket.

"I'm not so sure," she said and watched the tree change color from green to red and then a brilliant blue. A real pine would have been more suitable, but she hadn't the heart to dampen Cecily's enthusiasm for the modern optical version. Finding a tree at a store in the middle of the year had been a feat in itself.

"Wait until we stack the presents around it," her daughter said. "Then it will look real."

Fiona smiled. "Shall we do that now?" she asked, thinking of the stash of gifts in her spare room, all wrapped in assorted paper. Even Wyatt had given his niece some to put beneath her tree.

"Yes," Cecily said excitedly. "But you mustn't try and guess what I got for you. I tried to wrap it so it didn't look obvious."

Fiona crossed her fingers over her chest. "Cross my heart."

"Or Uncle Wyatt's to you," she said, and Fiona

stilled at the mention of him. "I told him to wrap it different, but he's too sensible for all that."

"Mmm. So let's get these gifts."

Fifteen minutes later, all the gifts were around the tree. The gift Wyatt had bought her was obviously professionally wrapped. The flat, two-foot-square object was intriguing, and she did her best not to grope the shiny bronze paper.

"Um...Fiona," Cecily said once the tree was sorted and they were in the backyard, playing with Muffin and drinking sodas. "Have you and Uncle Wyatt had a fight?"

Fiona stalled midsip but quickly gathered her wits. "Of course not. Why?"

Cecily tossed Muffin her toy. "I don't know... he just seems really cranky."

Yeah, cranky because she wouldn't talk to him. And probably cranky because she wouldn't sleep with him, either. After her shocking behavior in the kitchen, she could barely look at him. Loving him was one thing; acting so outrageously needy just because he said she was beautiful and looked at her as if she was the only woman on earth, well, that was another thing altogether.

But she was right to send him away. Fiona loved him—but she loved Cecily, too, and was determined to do what was best for her daughter. Falling in love with Wyatt wasn't sensible, and she would inevitably end up nursing a broken heart. And right now she didn't want to think about how he was feeling. It was simply too hard.

"I'm sure he's fine."

Cecily tossed the toy again. "I'm not so sure. If you guys have had a fight, couldn't you just make up or something?"

Guilt hit Fiona between the shoulders. "I promise I'll—"

"Everyone was angry that last Christmas at Waradoon," Cecily said quietly and dumped the toy because Muffin lost interest. "You know, the one before my parents died. I wasn't supposed to know, of course. But like I wouldn't know they were hardly talking to one another. And Uncle Wyatt was mad about something, too. He didn't even come to our house that year on Christmas Eve like he always did. My mother didn't kiss my dad under the plastic mistletoe. My dad sat in the corner and didn't say a word. And the worst thing about it was everyone kept telling me everything was fine. Well, *fine* just doesn't cut it anymore. So if it's not fine, I'd rather you told me the truth."

There was so much pain in her daughter's voice, and Fiona wanted nothing more than to soothe her. Cecily had lost so much. She wasn't about to let her own lack of control and foolishness impact her child in any way.

"I promise you that we really are fine. He's coming here tomorrow night for our Christmas-in-July thing, right? So, if we were fighting then he wouldn't be. We just needed some time apart this week. It's not a big deal," she added when Cecily raised both her brows. "Don't read too much into it. The fact is all I want to do is spend as much time as I can with you while you're here."

Cecily considered her words and nodded

slowly. "I want that, too. But I want you guys to like each other."

"We do. I promise." And it wasn't a lie. She did like Wyatt. The problem was she also loved him, and that seemed a whole lot more complicated than she could handle. "Adult relationships can be complex."

Cecily stared at her. "Because of sex?"

Fiona almost swallowed her tongue. "Er—yes...and because when two people like one another in that way, things get complicated."

"So you like Uncle Wyatt in that way?"

As things plummeted fantastically downhill, Fiona wanted to cover her ears. A mother-daughter sex talk she hadn't prepared for. "Well, the point I was trying to make is that sex isn't something to rush into with someone."

Cecily grinned. "Is this the part where you tell me I'm too young to think about it and should steer clear of all boys until I'm twenty-one?" She laughed and scooped the dog into her arms. "Uncle Wyatt has already given me that talk. His ears were red when he was saying it, which was pretty funny. Anyway, I think he was happy when I told him I wasn't interested in all that stuff yet. I know he said it because he doesn't want me to get into trouble and wreck my life."

Fiona's throat tightened. Cecily's words hit with the precision of an arrow. And they both knew it.

"Um—sorry," she said quickly. "I didn't mean that you'd wrecked your life or anything."

"It's okay," Fiona said assuredly. "I've never, not for one minute, regretted having you."

Cecily tried to smile. "Did you love him? I mean, my father?"

Fiona's heart thundered. *I'm not ready for this.* But Cecily deserved an answer.

"I didn't know him very well." That wasn't a lie. Jamie Corbett had been Shayne's lover for less than a month before the night they'd been left alone together. Shayne should have known better. And Fiona, starved of attention for so long, hadn't realized her harmless flirting was not harmless at all. Jamie Corbett mistook her clumsy attempt to get his attention, and it wasn't long before she endured the worst hour of her life. Afterward, sore and bruised and ashamed, Fiona vowed she'd never tell anyone what had happened. When Shayne discovered Fiona was pregnant, it didn't occur to her mother that her own lover was the father. Not until Fiona told her mother the truth. A truth Shayne didn't believe—instead she'd called Fiona every kind of tramp and accused her of trying to steal her boyfriend. Twenty-four hours later, Fiona was dumped at her uncle's farm, and she never saw Shayne or Jamie Corbett again.

She looked at Cecily and managed a smile. Her precious daughter wouldn't be tainted by the brutality and shame of her conception. Fiona would see to that with ever fiber of her being. "I was young and didn't have a lot of support at home. But if I hadn't met him, you wouldn't be here…and I wouldn't change that for the world."

Cecily's eyes glistened and she hugged the dog close. "I'm going to miss Muffin when I have to leave. Pop's got working dogs for the cattle and they're too big to pick up."

"I'm sure she'll miss you, too." *Like I will.* Fiona didn't dare let herself think about the day she would have to let her daughter go.

"You could come visit us at Waradoon."

She nodded, but in her heart she knew it wasn't likely. Her life was in Crystal Point. Cecily's life was at Waradoon. She would have to make do with school-vacation time to see her daughter. It would have to be enough.

Wyatt flipped his cell phone into his top pocket once he finished a call to his office. He and Cecily were due at Fiona's in an hour. He tried to ignore the anxiety filling his chest. He hadn't seen Fiona all week—at her request. He respected her wishes and didn't push the issue. Her impassioned words that morning were imprinted in his mind. She didn't want recriminations. She didn't want to discuss it. End of story.

But tonight was their Christmas-in-July celebration, and he didn't want to disappoint Cecily. Wyatt pushed past his battered ego and agreed they would spend the evening together.

It was near half past six when he stopped the rental car in her driveway behind her zippy Mazda. The porch light flickered and she opened the door as Cecily jumped out of the passenger seat. His niece was across the yard and up the three steps within seconds, and he watched as they embraced and Fiona dropped her head back as she laughed. His stomach rolled over. *Great start.*

He grabbed the bag from the backseat and headed for the two redheads in his life.

Cecily quickly disappeared inside, and to her credit, Fiona managed a smile as he approached. "Hi. Welcome."

"Thanks." He followed her across the threshold and closed the screen door. "Interesting tree," he said once they moved into the living room.

She shifted on her heels and her dress moved around her legs. "It's fiber-optic," she explained. "Cecily insisted."

"Saves having to store the decorations, I guess," he said and passed her the brown bag he carried. "From the organic deli in town."

She peered into the bag and bit her bottom lip as she examined the contents of Brie and crackers and antipasto ingredients. "Great, that's my favorite spot."

"I know," he replied. "Evie mentioned something."

She looked nervous all of a sudden. "Wyatt, I want to—"

"Hey, guys," Cecily announced as she bounced back into the room with Muffin in her arms. "Can we watch a Christmas DVD?"

Fiona sucked in a long breath. "Good idea. You pick a movie, and I'll get the drinks and snacks started."

She took off and Wyatt dropped into the love seat. He certainly had no intention of going anywhere near the sofa. He doubted he'd ever be able to look at the paisley print again without seeing Fiona stretched out in seductive invitation. And he wished she'd stop wearing that sexy perfume. Damn scent hit him with the force of a sledgehammer every time she came near him.

It was close to ten minutes before she came

back into the room. She did three trips and placed trays of food on the coffee table and drinks on the buffet nearby. He offered to help but she insisted she had it under control. She poured three glasses of something he couldn't distinguish, but which looked as if it had clumps of fruit in it, and placed them on the coffee table. When she was done, she sat in one corner of the sofa. Cecily sat in the middle and demanded he sit on the other side.

"You won't see the television from there," his niece complained. "I know how much you *looove* Christmas movies."

Wyatt looked toward Fiona. She smiled and flicked her gaze to the other end of the sofa. *Get a grip.* He moved and sat down, feeling light-years away from her.

"Not a fan, huh?" she asked and grabbed a handful of popcorn from the bowl in Cecily's lap.

"You could say that."

"Me, either," she admitted as the movie credits began to roll.

Cecily shushed them both and sat forward to pocket some chocolate. Then she slid off the edge, sat lotus-style in between the sofa and table, and began to graze on the selection of fruit and cheese and assorted food spread out in front of her.

Wyatt looked at Fiona. Being with her seemed incredibly normal. That was what struck him so hard. And so unexpectedly. She was easy to be with. Easy to like. What had started as physical attraction had morphed into something else. And the feelings were alien to him. He was somehow vulnerable.

Was that what mind-blowing sex did to a man's brain?

He reached across the back of the sofa and lightly touched her shoulder. She smiled as only she could. Wyatt wished he knew her better. He also wished he wasn't cynical and could trust what he was feeling. But he didn't. And he suspected Fiona knew as much.

Chapter Nine

Family.

That's what this feels like.

A mother, a father, a cheerful teenager plonked between them downing popcorn and laughing at a silly movie. Fiona knew it was a fantasy. But in that moment, it was real. And it was hers.

Wyatt's touch was mesmerizing. His hand stayed at her shoulder for a while, and he drew tiny circles with his thumb. She knew she shouldn't allow it. But it seemed right, somehow. When she moved to take her drink off the table, he pulled back.

Once the movie was over, Cecily insisted on opening a gift. Just one, she said, to tide them over until the following day. Her daughter's insistence that they follow the traditional Christmas protocol made her smile. Fiona sat on the love seat and summoned the heart to enjoy the celebration. Wyatt took a spot on an old chair next to the tree, and her daughter dropped onto the floor. Cecily opened one of the gifts Fiona gave her—a silver pendant in the shape of a dazzling unicorn. She adored it, thought it was the most beautiful thing she'd ever seen.

"It's one of a kind," Fiona explained. "My friend Mary-Jayne is a silversmith."

"A talented lady," Wyatt said and admired the piece.

"She's Evie's little sister. I'll get her to craft a pair of matching earrings," she told Cecily. "For your birthday."

Cecily groaned. "But that's ages away."

Fiona looked at Wyatt. "I know the date," she said and quickly changed the subject. "So, who's next?"

Cecily grabbed a gift from beneath the tree and tossed it toward her uncle. He squeezed the package. "Socks?"

Cecily laughed. "Nope. Fiona said they were off the list this year."

He mouthed a silent thank-you and tore open the gift. Not socks but a soft blue T-shirt she knew would look great on him.

"Now you," Cecily insisted and dragged the square package that was leaning against the wall.

Fiona rested the gift against her knees. They were both watching her—the child she loved and the man she had fallen hopelessly in love with.

The gift was from Wyatt, and as she pulled off the paper and realized what he'd given her, Fiona's eyes welled with tears. The portrait of Cecily was an exact likeness, framed in polished oak. "Oh…it's so…" She looked at Wyatt. "It's perfect. How did you—"

"Ellen," he explained. "My sister is the artist. She did this piece a few months back. I thought you might like it."

"I love it," she said quickly. *I love you.* "Thank you. It's more than I ever expected."

"Gosh, I look like you," Cecily said as she came behind Fiona and peered at the portrait. "Don't I, Uncle Wyatt?"

He kept his gaze locked with hers. "Yes. Double trouble."

Cecily laughed. It was such a heart-wrenching moment, and Fiona wanted to bottle up the memories. For another day, another time, when she was alone again.

"Who's up for supper?" she asked and blinked at the tears in her eyes.

"Not me," Cecily groaned out as she patted her full tummy. "Too much punch and popcorn. I think I'm going to crash for a while in the spare room."

She left with a hug for them both and took off down the short hallway.

"She exhausts me," Fiona declared as she slumped back in the love seat.

He grinned and checked his watch. "Nine-thirty," he commented. "And now we have no chaperone. Would you like me to leave?"

"No," she said in a rush and then exhaled. "I mean, we hardly need a chaperone."

He shrugged. "I'm not so sure."

Fiona did her best to ignore the simmering heat low in her belly. But in low-rise jeans and a black Henley shirt, he looked so good, so handsome, it was impossible to forget how passionately they'd made love only days earlier.

"I told you why I can't do this," she said quietly.

Wyatt stood up. "I know what you said. I'm just not entirely sure that's how you feel."

Fiona sucked in a sharp breath. Did he know she had fallen in love with him? *Am I that transparent?* "I have to put Cecily first. Not myself."

"So you said."

"You're leaving in ten days, Wyatt. I might come across as independent and self-sufficient, but the truth is I'm not the kind of woman who thinks it's okay to sleep with someone casually."

His expression narrowed. "I'm not indiscriminate, either, Fiona. I've had one brief relationship since I broke up with Yvette. I don't sleep around."

"I wasn't suggesting you—"

"I have no intention of ignoring you for the next ten days," he said quietly. "I'd like it if you showed me the same courtesy."

Shame weighed down her shoulders. He was right. She had been ignoring him. "I'm sorry. My only excuse is I'm afraid of messing things up with Cecily."

"You won't," he assured her. "Have some faith in yourself, Fiona. And trust Cecily."

"I've never been very good at trusting people."

Wyatt moved across the room and dropped onto the sofa. "Not surprising."

She shrugged. "I suppose. I did try to love my mother. But I didn't trust her to make the right choices." She gave a brittle laugh. "And she rarely let me down. I can't remember how many times I was dragged out of hotel rooms at dawn because she didn't have the money to pay the bill. Or how many cowboys she rolled over while they were asleep. I used to watch her steal money from their pockets and she'd tell me to be quiet when I begged her not to do it. Bad hotel rooms, short spells in one school or another... I never had the opportunity to make friends. And there was no point when we moved around so much. When she died, I think a part of me was...was..."

"Relieved?"

Fiona nodded and marveled at how easy it was to tell him things she'd always kept to herself. Not even Callie and Evie knew so much about her childhood.

This is it. This is trust. This is love.

"I'm not proud to think like that, but it's true. My uncle...well, he tried. He did the best he could, the best he knew how, I suppose. That's why it's so important I make the right choices now. I want Cecily to know I'm not a screwup."

"Acting on our mutual attraction doesn't make you a screwup, Fiona."

"Maybe," she said in a halfhearted sort of agreement. "All I know is that I am determined to be a good role model. I know in my heart your sister will always be her mother. I only hope I can be Cecily's friend, the woman she goes to when she needs guidance. Soon she'll be thinking about boys and love and sex. When she asks those questions, I want to be able to tell her that making love should be special…should be shared between two people who are *in love*."

Fiona looked at him, hoping, dreaming and wishing for some sign that he thought that, too. She'd made love with him because she loved him. Clearly for Wyatt it was little more than attraction. Mutual attraction, he'd called it. Not love. Only sex.

"You're right, of course," he said after a moment, and Fiona wished she knew what his impassive, locked-out expression meant. "And she should talk to you about that stuff."

"As long as I steer her in the right direction?"

His mouth twisted. "I want her to realize her potential. Be whoever she's meant to be."

"I want that, too. And again, I apologize for being shut down this week. We were both part of what happened. I didn't mean to make a bigger deal of it than it was. I don't want there to be tension between us. Especially since Cecily picked up on it."

"She did?"

"Yeah. She doesn't want us to fight. She doesn't like arguing." Fiona inhaled and met his gaze head-on. "Her parents fought in the few months before their deaths. I know you said it was nothing, but it meant something to Cecily. She's still disturbed by it."

"I'll talk to her," he said and shifted in his seat. "So, how about that supper you promised?"

"Hungry?"

He glanced at the remnants of food on the coffee table. "A man cannot live by popcorn alone. Allow me into your kitchen and I'll make you a sandwich you'll never forget."

Fiona laughed and then jumped up and straightened her dress over her hips. "Deal."

Fifteen minutes later, after she cleared away the scraps from the living room, Wyatt had loaded a plate with sandwiches filled with thick slices of ham and sweet pickles and a few with smoked turkey breast and cranberry jelly. He popped the plate in the center of the table, and Fiona grabbed two bottles of ginger beer from the refrigerator.

"Looks great," she said and sat down.

Wyatt grabbed a sandwich and devoured it in four bites.

There was an easy camaraderie between them. She liked it. Men usually made her nervous. But she had no nerves. Not even the underlying thread of sexual desire curling around the room made her tense. He wouldn't act on it; she knew that without question. He would respect her wishes. Wyatt oozed integrity by the bucket load.

"I guess we should talk about contact," she said after a few bites of her sandwich. "With Cecily. I would like to see her again on the next school vacation if that's okay with you."

He grabbed another sandwich. "You can see as much of Cecily as she wants."

Fiona's heart rolled. "Thank you for being so supportive. It means a lot to me."

"Cecily wants you in her life," he said around a bite. "Incidentally, you are welcome to visit Waradoon anytime. My mother will want to meet you. Sooner would be better than later."

Now Fiona was nervous. "Will she disapprove?"

"Of you?" He gave a lopsided grin. "Hardly."

Relief washed over her skin. "I'd like that."

Wyatt drank some ginger beer and patted his washboard-flat stomach. "I should probably check on Cecily. If she's crashed out, she may as well stay the night."

"Of course."

He stood and scraped the chair back. "Then I'll head off."

Fiona quickly got to her feet. "You could stay," she said and saw both his brows crank upward. "I mean, the sofa's pretty comfortable, and Cecily will want you to be here in the morning when she wakes up. And…I'd like that, too."

His mouth twisted and he went to say something, then stopped and took a moment. "If you're sure."

"I'm sure," she said quickly, before she had a chance to change her mind. "I'll get you a blanket and pillow."

He flexed his arms upward and stretched. The movement pulled the T-shirt up and exposed his belly. Fiona swallowed the sudden lump that formed in her throat. She'd touched him there, kissed him and reveled in his glorious skin. Her fingers itched as the memory swept through her blood.

Fiona took off to collect what he needed and detoured to check on Cecily. As expected, her daughter was asleep, snoring softly with Muffin curled in the crook of her arm. She called the dog, and once Muffin had jumped off the bed and shot past her feet, Fiona covered Cecily with a light blanket and flicked off the corner lamp.

Back in the living room, Fiona faced Wyatt.

I could so easily invite him into my bed.

The temptation heightened her awareness. She wanted him so much she could barely breathe.

She quickly dumped the pillow and blanket on the edge of the sofa. "Are you sure you'll be—"

"I'll be fine. Go to bed."

His words had a profound effect on her senses. "But if you need—"

"Go to bed," he said again, deeper this time. "Before I forget my good intentions."

Fiona stepped back, her heart pounding. She wanted him so much. Needed him so much. Loved him so much. Denying it suddenly seemed foolish. "I want you to stay," she whispered. "With me."

And within seconds she was in his arms.

The sofa wasn't comfortable, as Wyatt discovered around 4:00 a.m. when he left Fiona asleep and made his way to the living room. Her big bed, with its colorful quilt and plump pillows, was a much more appealing option— especially since Fiona's lovely arms had been wrapped around him. But he'd been struck by a burst of doing the right thing. And that meant being settled on the couch when Cecily woke up.

So he stared at the ceiling for two hours, in between shooing off the dog that clearly wanted to curl up between his feet.

Last night, despite his best intentions, the moment she'd walked into his arms, Wyatt had crumbled. Her skin, her lips and her beautiful hair—he had no answer for the burning desire that consumed him whenever she was near him. He couldn't resist. No woman had ever had such an effect on him. There had been no words when they'd made love. Only touch and taste and an exploration of the senses. Each stroke more mind-blowing than the last.

Wyatt groaned and put the pillow over his face to muffle the sound. He swung his legs off the sofa and sat up. Sleep was out of the question. Television filled the next hour or so, and at dawn he heard Cecily's cheerful voice echoing down the hallway.

Fiona emerged about ten minutes later, and by then he was in the kitchen making coffee. Dressed in pale-gray-and-black, sweats she looked weary and sleep-deprived. And so beautiful his breath caught in his throat.

"Coffee. Mmm…lovely," she said and took the mug he offered.

Cecily was bouncing around within seconds. "Merry Christmas in July!" She hugged them both. "Oh, can we please open gifts first?"

Wyatt caught Fiona's gaze. There would be no holding back his exuberant niece and they both knew it. "Sure," Fiona said. "Lead the way."

It took about three minutes for Cecily to devour all her gifts and leave a pile of discarded wrapping paper in her wake as she danced on happy feet, clinging to the new cell phone he'd given her. A good idea he'd be sure to thank Fiona for suggesting.

Sharing gifts with Fiona seemed ridiculously intimate, and he knew Cecily watched them interact with keen interest. His niece was hoping, he suspected, to see their relationship develop into something more, something permanent. Wyatt knew she wanted to be a part of a traditional family unit again. And Fiona was her birth mother—in Cecily's young eyes it would be the perfect solution.

Would he consider it? When he knew it would mean a commitment and ultimately marriage? He couldn't deny his attraction for Fiona. And they were compatible in many ways. Not only between the sheets. He liked her and enjoyed her company. But his resistance lingered. He'd been played before. How could he be sure this wouldn't turn out the same?

"If it's not detailed enough, I can return it."

Wyatt shifted his attention to the moment. Fiona was watching him as he handled the thick book on car restoration, and he remembered how he'd mentioned he had plans to one day rebuild the '67 Camaro his father had in the garage at Waradoon.

"It's great," he replied. "Thanks."

She looked at the book and grimaced. "You're difficult to buy for."

"I told you he had everything," Cecily chimed in as she took a second away from her phone.

"Imagine trying to come up with something new every year…*sheesh*."

"Do you have everything?" Fiona asked quietly once Cecily returned to pressing buttons.

Wyatt held her gaze. "Right now…I think I do."

And suddenly Wyatt knew his orderly, practical life would be empty without Fiona Walsh in it.

The day had a surreal edge for Fiona. By midmorning she'd cooked breakfast, which they shared around the kitchen table, as they chatted through mouthfuls of fried ham and eggs. Afterward, Wyatt helped her wash the dishes. Before she had a chance to protest, Fiona found herself trapped between his chest and the kitchen counter and caught in a delicious lip-lock with him that was so passionate it made her heart surge. Of course, Cecily catching them in a clinch as she walked into the kitchen had Fiona pulling away so quickly she almost fell over. This made her daughter laugh, and Wyatt grab her with lightning-fast reflexes before she ended up in a twisted heap on the floor.

Her embarrassment aside, the time she spent with them both would become bottled memories she'd treasure forever. Cecily's animated happiness was almost too sweet to bear. And Wyatt... She wished she knew what the future held. Especially after last night. She'd spouted a whole lot of reasons why they couldn't get involved and then rushed into his arms again. Fiona cursed her lack of self-control. But still, he was such a wonderful lover—thoughtful and attentive, passionate and reverent. She'd discovered more about giving and receiving pleasure in the past week than she had in all her adult life.

But what was he feeling? She wanted to believe he genuinely cared for her and to believe it was more than a fling. His comments while they'd opened gifts that morning encouraged her to think he did. But without the actual words, how could she be sure? Assurance had never seemed more important. He liked her...she was savvy enough to figure that out. And they were good together in bed. *So good. Too good.* So good her hormones were running riot. But sex wasn't enough to sustain a relationship between two people who hardly knew one another. And with Cecily clearly hoping for it to happen, Fiona knew her daughter would be painfully disappointed if they started something that faded as quickly as it had begun. Cecily had endured enough disappointments, and Fiona wasn't about to add to the load.

By eleven she said goodbye and waved farewell to them from the front porch when they returned to the B and B to change clothes. There was a baby shower at Evie's parents' home that afternoon, and since they'd all been invited, they'd agreed to go together. Like a real family.

Exactly the family I've longed for.

But she needed reality. She also refused to let her imagination run away with wild ideas. After she showered and changed into a knee-length pale blue dress cut on the bias, Fiona waited for about ten minutes before they returned to pick her up.

Wyatt looked so good in chinos and a white shirt it stole her breath.

"Ready?" he asked as she opened the door.

"Yes," she said quickly. "I just have this to take." She picked up a bag near the door. "Makings for a cheese-and-fruit platter and a gift for Evie and Scott's baby," she explained.

She didn't pull back when he grabbed the bag in one hand and took her hand with the other. Once Fiona had closed the door, he walked her to the car. Cecily was grinning from ear to ear in the backseat. *Oh, no...don't start thinking this is something real.* She wanted to say the words out loud. To herself. To her daughter. Knowing how it must look with their hands linked, Fiona pulled away as they reached the car and quickly ducked into the front seat. He placed the bag in the back and they headed off.

The trip to the Prestons' home took only a few minutes, and by the time they arrived, there were several cars parked outside. Cecily jumped out quickly before Fiona had a chance to move and took off to find Lily. Wyatt reached across and grasped her arm.

"Fiona?"

"Everyone's inside," she breathed. "Let's go—"

"I think we should talk."

She knew what was coming, didn't she? The talk. The let's-be-friends speech. She'd heard it before. Maybe she'd imagined his interest as being more than sexual? Whatever it was, she was going down fast. And she had to save herself.

"You want out?" she blurted and moved her arm.

"What?"

"From me…from whatever this is."

He frowned. "Why would I want that?"

Fiona shrugged. "Because it's less complicated."

"If I didn't want complicated," he said and grabbed her hand, "I wouldn't have come here to find you in the first place. I would have told Cecily to wait until she was eighteen and search for you then. But I did come here and we did meet…and we did connect."

Connect? God, she should be jumping out of her skin that he wasn't backing out. Instead, her heart was thumping so hard she wondered if she would hyperventilate. She wanted more than a connection. She wanted *I love you*. He stroked her hand with his thumb and watched her with blistering intensity, and it wasn't enough. It would never be enough. She wanted the lot. She wanted him in every way possible.

"But you're leaving soon."

"Yes," he replied and kept stroking her skin. "I have to get back. The company, my family. It's all a long way from here."

Fiona nodded because she wasn't sure she could do anything else.

"So, come to Waradoon?"

"But I—"

"And soon. Let's see if this connection works somewhere else."

God, she was tempted. "Cecily would—"

"Think it's a great idea," he said, cutting her off without batting an eye.

Of course she would. Cecily wanted a family. With parents and siblings one day. She hadn't dared admit to her daughter that it was her dream, too. But what about Wyatt's dreams? His fiancée had cheated on him—could she expect that he'd want to get seriously involved with anyone?

"I don't know. I'll think about it."

He didn't look happy with her response, but after a second, he shrugged. "Sure. We should go inside, don't you think?"

Fiona agreed and quickly got out of the car. Wyatt retrieved the bags from the backseat and she waited for him by the bottom step. Once inside, she took the bags from him and headed for the kitchen and left Wyatt to his own devices, presumably to hang out with the rest of the men and talk about the stuff men seemed to be able to talk about even if they weren't well acquainted.

Callie was in the kitchen cutting thick slices of watermelon, and Evie was decorating a fluffy meringue. Both women eyed Fiona as she walked into the room, and Callie raised her brows. Fiona knew that look—knew her friend had something on her mind.

"What?"

Callie wasn't one to beat around the bush. "Cecily just made an appearance. Where's the gorgeous uncle?"

Fiona dumped the bags on the counter. "Outside. And I'd rather not—"

"She's onto you."

"Huh?"

Callie's mouth turned up at the edges. "Cecily. She and Lily have become firm friends. She told Lily that you and Wyatt were, and I quote, 'so doing it.'"

Fiona's cheeks burned. "Lily said that?"

"Yes. Our girls have been texting in the small hours. They've got quite the hotline going." Callie stopped her cutting.

Evie spoke. "So, is it true?"

Fiona opened her mouth in protest. But this was Callie and Evie. Her best friends. "We're… well…yes."

"Good for you," Evie said and smiled.

Callie didn't look so pleased. "I thought you didn't want to complicate things?"

"I don't. Anyway, it won't last," she said and despised how foolishly hopeless she sounded.

Callie looked at her. "You're sure of that?"

"I'm not sure of anything," Fiona admitted. "What I'm feeling. What Wyatt's feeling. If he's feeling anything at all. And with Cecily stuck in the middle, it's getting harder every day. I have absolutely no idea what I'm doing here."

Callie looked serious suddenly. "Well, considering what happened with her parents, I think you need to figure it out. You can tell me to mind my own business, but I think the last thing that girl needs is more confusion in her life."

Fiona frowned. "What do you mean?"

"Well, despite her obvious exuberance for the two of you to be together, Cecily isn't entirely convinced any relationship can survive since she found out about her father's affair."

Fiona stilled, poleaxed by Callie's words. "Her father's *what?*"

"Affair," Callie said again and looked at her oddly. "She told Lily. I was sure she would have said something to you."

"No. Only that they were having some problems." The words left her mouth with a kind of static disbelief. "Are you sure that's what she said?"

Callie nodded. "He'd had an affair. Apparently they'd gone away together on a trip to work on their marriage. Since they were killed the day before they were due to arrive home, I guess no one will ever know whether they were able to work things out."

An affair?

Fiona couldn't believe it. Oh, not that Jim Todd had been unfaithful. But that Wyatt hadn't told her. She'd asked him about his sister's marriage, and he'd shrugged off her questions and shut her out. Deliberately. And she wouldn't stand for it. Not with Cecily stuck in the middle.

Fiona knew she had to start thinking with her head and not her heart.

Or I might lose everything.

And that, she thought with a resolute breath, was not an option.

Chapter Ten

Wyatt sensed the distinct change in Fiona's mood the moment she walked outside. She glared at him with a kind of unholy rage as she walked across to where Cecily sat by the pool. He wished he knew her better. He hung out with Noah and Cameron for a while and saw his chance to speak with her when she made her way back into the house. He followed her through the kitchen and into the front living room. She clearly knew he was behind her because her back was stiff with tension.

"Fiona, wait up."

She stalled about ten feet in front of him and turned. "What?"

He took note of her bright blue-gray eyes and lips pressed tight. "Exactly—what?"

She opened her mouth and then quickly clamped it shut.

"What's wrong?" he insisted.

"Now isn't the time to get into it."

"Seems like the perfect time."

"In someone else's home?" She shook her head. "I don't think so."

"So, all this sudden anger is aimed at me?"

She rocked back on her heels. "At myself," she said and flicked her hair in that way he could not ignore. "For being so gullible."

"Gullible?" Wyatt stepped closer and shut the sliding door. "What does that mean?"

"It means that I've become so wrapped up in *wanting* you I've forgotten why you're here. I've forgotten what I'm doing. I've also forgotten that I promised this would only be about Cecily."

Wyatt pushed past his frustration and tried to not sound impatient. "That's something of an old song, don't you think? We can't undo what's done."

Her blue-gray eyes flashed lightning. "Well, you would say that, considering you've been moving me around like a pawn on a chessboard."

He stared at her. "What?"

"Lying by omission is still lying," she said hotly, as if she couldn't get the words out quickly enough.

Annoyance ignited behind his ribs. He had no idea what she meant. "I haven't lied to you."

Both her brows shot up. "Really? So, if letting me think your sister's marriage was rock-solid, when we both know it wasn't, isn't lying, what is?"

Wyatt swayed fractionally. "What are you talking about?"

"You know exactly," she shot back. "Your sister and her husband were having a few problems, you said. Nothing serious. Since when is infidelity nothing?"

Infidelity? So, she knew. He wondered how

much. "Since it's a private family issue and none of your business."

Wyatt knew it sounded harsh and dismissive. And he knew she'd be hurt by his words. But he wasn't about to lay any Harper skeletons out for open discussion. The past was the past, and that was exactly where it would remain. Even if it meant shutting her out.

She took a heavy breath. "And that puts me in my place? Well, I'm pleased we've cleared that up. I'd hate to harbor the illusion that I was important enough to be privy to something about your family. Or you."

Her eyes flashed at him. He could have said something to assure her she was important. Or that she was quickly becoming the most important thing to him. Instead he stuck by his determination to keep the whole ugly mess from hurting any more people than it already had.

"What happened in my family has no bearing on your relationship with Cecily."

It sounded exclusive and they both knew it.

"What about my relationship with you?" she asked, suddenly all eyes, all emotion.

Wyatt wasn't sure where their relationship was heading. It was too new. Too raw. And arguing about it wouldn't help. "It's nothing—"

"Nothing?" Her voice rose as she cut him off.

"If you'd let me finish—"

"Oh, we're finished all right," she said and glared at him. "We are absolutely finished. Over. Done. *Kaput.*"

"You're overreacting," he replied, harsher than he liked.

"What does it matter? We've already established that I'm nothing to you."

Wyatt expelled a frustrated breath. "That's not what I said."

"I know exactly what you—"

"Would you stop fighting? Just stop!"

They both stilled. Cecily had emerged from the hall and stood in the doorway, her eyes bright and her cheeks red. When they said her name simultaneously, she shook her head with a kind of frantic denial.

"Just stop fighting…please," she implored and wrapped her thin arms around herself.

Guilt hit Wyatt in the center of his chest. He remembered those last few months before Karen and Jim were killed. It had been a tough time, and Cecily had been in the middle of it, as much as he knew his sister had done her best to shield her from seeing and hearing too much. "We were just—"

"Fighting," she wailed. "Arguing."

Fiona stepped toward her. "I'm sorry if you thought we were—"

"I heard you. I know what fighting sounds like."

"And you're right," Wyatt said quietly and tried to ignore the pain of Fiona's expression and the confusion on his niece's face. "But it wasn't about you. It wasn't anything to do with you. So nothing has changed for you, Cecily. Fiona and I are both here for you. That's all that matters."

"You were talking about my folks," Cecily said. "I heard. And I know what Dad did."

Did she? Wyatt wondered if she knew everything. If she knew the role he'd played in the whole sordid mess. Karen had blamed him often enough. When Wyatt had suggested that she and her husband take some time out to get their relationship back on track and see if they could make their marriage work, he hadn't imagined it would be the last time they'd speak.

"They loved you. Your dad loved you. Don't worry about anything else."

His niece shrugged and stepped back, away from Fiona, away from him. "I thought things would work out," Cecily said shakily. "This morning you guys were... Well, I thought we'd all be together and happy."

"Cecily," he said gently, "Fiona and I are friends and we'll do our best to remain friends. But relationships can be complex."

"I've already had the adult-relationships-are-complicated speech from her," she said and pointed a finger in Fiona's direction. "If it's so complicated, why did you sleep together in the first place?"

Wyatt saw Fiona turn pale and fought the urge

to go to her. And Cecily looked as if she needed comfort, too. By chance and circumstance, they had become the most important people in his life. If Karen and Jim were alive, they would be doing this. They would be standing guard over the reunion between birth mother and daughter. And he'd be living his own life, perhaps only involved peripherally. But his sister was gone. It was his job to protect Cecily. And because he and Fiona were lovers, because they'd crossed the line from acquaintance into friendship and then into something way more intimate than he'd bargained for, he experienced a deep-rooted need to protect Fiona, as well. And knowing how important the moment was to both of the women standing in front of him, Wyatt quickly shouldered the responsibility.

"Because when you're falling for someone that's what people do. And sometimes guys can act like jerks when it comes to a beautiful woman."

Cecily's mouth opened in a rounded O.

Of all things Fiona might have expected Wyatt

to say, that wasn't one of them. She stared at him and then glanced at her daughter. Cecily's face creased in a tiny smile.

"So, you guys are cool?"

"Yes," he replied quietly.

Fiona was so angry with him she hurt all over. But she wouldn't say another word in front of Cecily. She'd done enough damage to their relationship for one day.

"We're fine," she said flatly. "And friends, just as your uncle said."

"Good. Fighting sucks. What if you fight and then something happens and you never see that person again?"

So young and so smart. Her daughter was a remarkable young woman. She had some serious ground to make up after allowing her personal feelings for Wyatt to blur what was really important.

Fiona looked toward Wyatt for a bare second. *Because when you're falling for someone that's what people do.* Did he mean it? Was he really falling for her? Had he guessed she'd fallen completely and hopelessly in love with him? No. Impossible. He wasn't falling. She was *nothing* to him. He'd only said that to appease Cecily. More lies.

"How about you and I go and check out what Callie and Lily are doing?" She linked her arm through her daughter's and hoped Cecily would accept her embrace.

She did, thankfully. "Great idea. Are you coming, Uncle Wyatt?"

"No, you go ahead. I want to finish talking with Lily's dad about the school canteen project."

Fiona managed to look at him again. "He's going to help?"

"Looks that way," Wyatt replied.

"He has three kids at the school, so I'm not surprised."

Wyatt shrugged in a vague kind of way, which belied the tension radiating from him. They needed to talk and they both knew it. But now wasn't the time or place.

"Noah has contacts in the local building industry and can assist with organizing contract labor from this end," Wyatt said. "Your funds from Harper's should be cleared within thirty days, so once the plans are submitted and approved through council, the project can go ahead."

"Ooh," Cecily said with a burst of sudden excitement. "You'll have to come to the big Harper's charity ball next month. Won't she, Uncle Wyatt?"

His eyes regarded her with burning intensity. "Of course," he replied. "In fact, it's customary for a representative of the beneficiaries of the charity fund to attend. You could represent the school and accept your check on the night."

"Oh, I couldn't possibly—"

"It would be perfect," Cecily said excitedly. "You could stay at Waradoon and meet Nan and Pop and my aunts and everyone else. And don't forget Banjo. I really want you to see my horse. Please say you'll come and stay. We can go shopping for our dresses together. It's really fancy and so much fun." She turned her attention to her uncle. "Make her say yes, Uncle Wyatt."

He nodded. "You'd be welcome to attend."

It wasn't exactly the invitation from him she secretly craved. *I really want you to come with me* would have been better. Perhaps he already had a date? That thought made Fiona hurt all over. She cursed herself for being so foolish. They were finished. She was *nothing* to him.

"I'll think about it," she said, stiffer than she would have liked, and the disappointment on her daughter's face plunged into her heart like a knife. "I promise," she added. "Now, let's go and see Lily."

She steered Cecily from the room. There would be time later for recriminations. All she wanted was to enjoy the day with her daughter. And later, much later, she would think about how she would face Wyatt alone, knowing how little she meant to him and knowing he'd only said what he'd said to appease Cecily's concerns.

And it hurt more than she'd believed possible.

Fiona hadn't expected Cecily to want to stay the night at the Prestons'. But she and Lily had forged such a strong friendship, and Fiona didn't have the heart to deny her daughter's request. Wyatt didn't look happy about it but gave in when Cecily promised to be back at the B and B early the following morning.

The drive back to her house later that evening was thick with tension. She managed to avoid him for most of the afternoon and didn't say anything until Wyatt pulled the car into her driveway.

She grabbed her handbag and moved to open the door. "Well, thank you for the lift. Can you tell Cecily that I'll call her—"

"Fiona?"

She stopped moving when he spoke her name. "What?"

He expelled a sharp breath. "We need to talk, either now or later. I'd prefer now. I'd like an opportunity to explain my reasons for keeping my family's business private."

She knew why. She didn't need to hear it again. *Because I'm nothing to you.*

"Okay," she said as she opened the door. "Let's talk."

Minutes later they were inside. Fiona gave Muffin a moment's attention when the little dog bounded toward her, then she dropped her bags on the hall stand and headed for the living room. She heard Wyatt close the front door, and she was seated on the sofa by the time he'd traced her steps.

He remained standing, his shoulders tight and expression unreadable. "I didn't lie to you," he said quietly. "The fact is I didn't tell you about Karen and Jim's marriage problems because I didn't think it had any bearing on your relationship with Cecily."

Fiona drew in a breath. "You know, I'm not so naive I'd actually believe that hogwash."

He made an irritated sound. "So you're determined to think I did it deliberately?"

She nodded. "I think you did it because it was easier to keep me in the dark. It was easier to let me believe they were perfect."

"No one's perfect."

She shot up. "No? Well, you never gave me a chance, did you? Right from the beginning, from the moment we met and you told me about Cecily, I've been busting my behind trying to prove that I'm good enough...that I deserve to be a part of Cecily's life."

"I've never once asked you to aim for some perfect standard. In fact, I recall saying that Karen and Jim were *not* perfect."

"You didn't have to say anything either way," she snapped back. "It's been made clear to me that they were the faultless parents who loved Cecily. You made me believe they were flawless and as though I didn't have a hope of competing with that. So I tried to be myself...my very obviously *flawed* self and hoped that was enough."

"It is enough. Cecily is already attached to you."

"Because her perfect parents are gone. Don't you think I get that? If Karen were here, my relationship with Cecily would be very different."

Wyatt's gaze sharpened instantly. "What do

you expect? She lost her mother. She's looking for that connection again."

"I know that. I know what she wants and I'm trying so hard to give it to her. But if I'd known I might have been doing this on an even playing field, I could have, I don't know, worked out a way to not seem so *desperate* to make it work out. But I haven't. I'm the screwup who gave her away, and I'll always be that person."

"You're not a screwup, Fiona."

"I am," she shot back. "I gave her up. I handed her over to strangers. I abandoned her. And I know, in her heart, a part of Cecily is always going to think that. She's always going to know they wanted her and I didn't."

"You can't change the past. Believe me, I know that. And I know my niece. She's grateful to have you in her life. You want to hear than Karen and Jim weren't perfect, that their marriage was busted and they were on the verge of splitting? Sure, I can tell you that. I can tell you Jim slept with another woman and it broke my sister's heart. So, now you know, does it change anything about your relationship with Cecily? I don't think so. Unless you want to keep using it as an excuse to hide behind."

Fiona's skin prickled. "What?"

"An excuse," he said again. "In case you mess up with Cecily. It's an easy out for you, isn't it?"

"That's not fair. I've never—"

"Oh, come on, Fiona, you've got that blueprint down pat. I've read the report, remember? The moves from one town to the next, short stints as a contract teacher, a few brief relationships with men you never see again once the relationship fizzles out. You can't hide from the truth when it's written in black-and-white."

Anger and humiliation crept over her skin. "Black-and-white?" she echoed, incredulous and so fired up she almost lunged at him and smacked his face. "You knew? I mean, you know about—"

"The accountant? The truck driver? The real-estate salesman?"

Put that way, it sounded like a long list, and shame filled her blood. "I was in a committed relationship with each of..." She paused, re-grouped, tried to say the words without making herself feel cheap and indiscriminate. "What I meant is that I knew each of those men for well over six months before we moved our relationship to the next level. I've only once ever jumped into an intimate relationship without really knowing the person."

"You mean with Cecily's father?"

"I mean with you." Fiona pushed back her shoulders as the truth tumbled from her lips and she didn't care that he looked annoyed by her admission. "Actually, I didn't have a relationship with *him* at all."

Wyatt's eyes narrowed. "Then what was it? A one-night stand?"

Fiona's skin burned, and she felt as though her body were suddenly moving in exaggerated slow motion. If only it *had* been a one-night stand. As the color drained from her face, Fiona knew Wyatt was intensely aware of her altering demeanor. He was a smart guy. The truth teetered

on her lips and she swallowed hard. "It was…
it was…"

His expression changed quickly. She watched,
both fascinated and mortified, as he worked out
that something wasn't quite right. A familiar
deep-rooted shame washed across her skin.

"Fiona?"

She turned away from the soft sound of his
voice. After a few deep breaths, she found her
voice. "Jamie Corbett."

"What?"

"That's what you wanted to know, isn't it?"
she said and wrapped her arms across her chest.
"You wanted his name. Now you have it."

"Corbett?" She heard the query in his voice.
"Why does that sound so—"

"Familiar?" Fiona said on a shaky breath. "It
would be if you read the report on my mother's
death."

"I did," Wyatt replied steadily. "She was killed
in a train-crossing accident alongside her twenty-
two-year-old…" He stopped and took a few seconds. "Jamie Corbett was your mother's lover?"

Fiona shuddered. An image, like a speedy camera in reverse, flashed through her mind, and the memories leached into her skull. Shayne had gone out looking to score. Fiona was left alone in the grimy motel room they occupied with the young cowboy her mother had picked up in a bar a month earlier. He'd seemed friendly at first. So she'd smiled and crossed her legs as she sat propped up on the single bed she occupied. He'd joined her on the bed to play cards and they'd laughed together. She'd liked the attention, liked how he told her she was pretty and would grow up to be a real heartbreaker one day. He'd touched her ankle at first. Then her leg. When she'd pulled away, he'd grabbed her harder. Although still a virgin, Fiona had known enough about sex to realize what was about to happen.

"Fiona?" Wyatt's voice pulled her back into the present. "Are you saying that Corbett is Cecily's father?"

Emotion clutched her throat. "Yes."

He said her name softly. "Would you turn around?"

She did as he asked slowly, still holding her arms tightly around her chest. She could barely hold contact with his eyes. She focused on the tiny pulse in his cheek beating rapidly. She knew he was thinking, imagining and probably working her out.

But he didn't speak straightaway. When she did meet his gaze, there was a somber realization in his blue eyes. "Fiona, what did he do to you?"

Fiona closed her eyes for a moment and sucked in a breath. She hadn't said the words out loud since telling her mother she was pregnant a couple of months later. And Shayne hadn't believed her. Instead, Fiona had been accused of trying to run interference in her mother's relationship with Jamie Corbett and she'd been quickly shipped off to her uncle.

The words clawed at her throat and she swallowed hard. "He took… He was…"

As her admission trailed off, silence stretched

between them like brittle elastic. Finally, Wyatt spoke again. "Fiona, did he rape you?"

She shook her head and then nodded. "It was… Yes…I suppose…"

"Suppose?"

"Well," she managed to reply despite the hard lump in her throat, "I said no."

"And?"

Fiona didn't miss his quiet control and took a few moments before she replied. "And he said I'd asked for it. Said I wanted it. He said a lot of things." She dropped her arms and sat on the sofa. "Maybe in a way I did ask for it. I don't know what to think anymore. Shayne had left us alone in the motel room. I guess I was flattered at first… He paid me some attention, and with my mother the way she was, I was *starved* for it, if that makes sense."

It did make sense. But Wyatt could barely think straight as he absorbed what she was telling him. He pushed the building rage back down and tried to concentrate. "What did you do… after?"

She shrugged and looked so small and vulnerable, so alone, Wyatt had to force himself to remain where he was and not take her in his arms and offer her the comfort he suspected she desperately needed.

"My mother didn't believe me," she said softly. "When I found out I was pregnant, she accused me of trying to come between them. The next day I was sent to my uncle."

Wyatt clenched his fists. "You didn't press charges? You didn't make him—"

"I was fifteen," she said and drew in a heavy breath. "And afraid."

Rationally, and in that part of him that was civilized and logical, Wyatt understood. But that other part, the one that was fuelled by a powerful and instinctive urge to protect her, wanted to grind Corbett into the ground.

"And you've never told anyone what happened?"

She shook her head. "No. They were killed three weeks after I went to live with my uncle. Telling wouldn't have changed what happened.

Once Cecily was born, I didn't have a chance to think about anything other than how I had to give my baby away."

Wyatt's insides tightened into knots and he experienced a deep-rooted pain behind his ribs. There were so many people who should have been held accountable for what had happened to her—certainly the lowlife who had brutalized her and the mother who hadn't given a damn. There was the great-uncle, too…and even Karen, who had insisted on a closed adoption, knowing full well that Cecily's birth mother was only fifteen.

"You were let down badly by your family," he said, more statement than question.

She shrugged. "I guess I've never really had a family. Now, because of Cecily, for the first time in my life I feel like I have a chance to have one. And I don't want to do anything to ruin that chance. We jumped into bed together after only a week. We gave in to the attraction, but at the end of the day it's just sex. And sex isn't enough to sustain a relationship, not even great sex." She sighed heavily. "Let's face it, if it was something more, you would have trusted me enough to tell me about your sister's marriage being in trouble, right?"

The truth knocked against his rib cage. He didn't trust easily. Somehow Fiona knew that. "Karen's relationship with Jim had nothing to do with you and Cecily. I know you've worked hard to develop a relationship with Cecily. It has a strong foundation now and will only become stronger the more time you spend together."

Her eyes moistened. "What if she can't forgive me for giving her up?"

"She can," he replied gently. "She has. She cares about you. And I care about you, Fiona. But after the way things ended with Yvette, I'm not about to rush into something without being certain it's going to last. The fact that Cecily wants to see us together makes it even more important to take things slowly. That's why I asked you to come to Waradoon to meet the family. We need time to get to know one another outside of the bedroom, don't you think?"

"But if it fades…I mean, if the attraction we have for each other disappears, what then? What do I do, Wyatt? With Cecily stuck in the middle, how do we push past that?"

"You're predicting failure before we've barely begun?"

Fiona let out a heavy breath. "Because that's what I do. I fail at relationships. I'm nearly thirty years old and the longest friendships I've had are with Callie and Evie and we've only known one another a few years. And you, I imagine, with your picture-perfect family and private-school education—I'll bet you have the same friends you made in kindergarten."

He didn't deny it.

Emotion glittered in her eyes. "You're right about me. Each time a relationship ends, I shut down. I shut down because I don't want to be friends when it's over. Maybe it's some hang-up from watching my mother get ditched by one man after the other and how she tried to cling to them afterward and made a fool of her-self by trying to stay friends and keeping herself involved in their lives—even after they'd moved on."

Wyatt rocked back on his heels. "You're not your mother, Fiona."

The tears fell. She blinked a couple of times and drew in a shuddering breath so deep he felt it through to the marrow in his bones. Something uncurled in his chest, a strange and piercing pain that hit him with the sharpness of an arrow.

Wyatt wasn't sure how he ended up in front of her or how she ended up in his arms.

"But how do I ever tell her the truth, Wyatt?"

He held her close. "She'll understand. When you're ready, when she's ready...and I'll be there with you when you do."

"How can I be sure?"

He kissed the top of her head. "I know how much Cecily means to you and I'm not about to tear her out of your life. She's your daughter, Fiona. You're not alone anymore."

But Wyatt knew she didn't quite believe him.

Chapter Eleven

Saying goodbye to Cecily was the hardest thing Fiona had ever done. She'd had her three weeks and now it was over. Her heart felt as if it would shatter into a million pieces.

And saying goodbye to Wyatt just about tipped her over the edge. Exaggerated by the fact their relationship had gone from being lovers to Wyatt treating her like a protective big brother.

The intimacy was gone. He'd changed toward her. He was polite and caring and made an effort to spend time with her and Cecily, but she wasn't fooled. The politeness was excruciating.

The friendliness made her want to scream. The most intimate thing he did was grab her hand to help her up the stairs at the information kiosk when they visited the local turtle rookery. She'd told him everything. Her deepest secret. And he'd pulled away. It hurt so much she wasn't sure how she managed to get through the last few days.

Of course, they would still have contact. He was Cecily's guardian, and any decisions about contact with her daughter would have to be approved by Wyatt. But their relationship had become so lukewarm it was barely recognizable.

On the day she had to say goodbye, all her energy was focused on staying calm. Cecily didn't need to see her tears. As it was, her daughter hugged her so tightly she had to choke back a sob. When Wyatt kissed her on the cheek, she'd swayed against him a little, remembering, wanting to feel the safety in his arms once more before he left her.

"Thank you for everything," she whispered against his jaw as she pulled back.

He raised a brow. "Everything?"

"For bringing Cecily here," she explained. "For giving me this chance."

"It's been good for Cecily. I owe you thanks for welcoming her into your life."

With her heart breaking, she'd waved them off outside the B and B, watching as the rental car disappeared down the road. Evie came up behind her and dropped an arm over her shoulder.

"You okay?" her friend asked.

Fiona swallowed the lump in her throat. "Yeah."

"She's a remarkable girl."

Pride swelled in her chest. "I know."

"And the tall drink of water?" Evie asked as one brow rose dramatically.

"It's over," she replied and blinked the hotness from her eyes.

"You're in love with him?"

She didn't bother to deny it. "Crazy, huh?"

"To fall in love?" Evie shook her head. "Not at all. You're going to see them in a couple of weeks, right?"

She nodded. "Yes, for the charity dinner."

Everything was organized. She'd fly down for four days while Mary-Jayne stayed at her house to look after Muffin, and Callie would care for Titan. Cecily insisted they go shopping for their dresses in the city, and she was looking forward to scouring a few high-end boutiques for just the right gown to wear at the charity dinner.

"So, if you decide to stay, I'll understand."

Stay? Had she considered it? To leave Crystal Point would be a wrench. She loved her job, her friends and her little house. But to be close to Cecily...the idea filled her with immense joy.

"My life is here, though."

"Home is where the heart is," Evie replied and squeezed her shoulders assuringly. "Your daughter needs you. And Wyatt, I suspect, needs you, too...even if he doesn't know it yet."

"So, Cecily tells me you and the birth mother got kind of close during the big visit?"

Wyatt glared at his sister. Ellen, as usual, always said exactly what was on her mind.

"She has a name. And it's none of your business."

"Ha—don't get all brooding and silent on me. I think it's great. Cecily certainly approves of the match."

The match? Was that what it was? Stupid. They hardly knew one another.

But he missed her like hell. And he walked around like a bear with a sore head. His family was too polite to really say anything intrusive about his increasingly obvious bad mood. Only Glynis, his assistant, told him to take a pill for whatever ailed him.

"Cecily wants a mother again," he remarked and smiled when Ellen's daughter grabbed hold of his knees and thrust a squishy, dog-eared picture book in his direction.

"What Cecily wants is a mother and a father who love one another."

Wyatt looked at his sister for a moment and then hauled not-quite-two-year-old Amy into his arms. "We'll see what happens," he said and flipped open the book as Amy pumped her chubby legs.

Ellen huffed. "Not all women are like Yvette."

He glanced up. "I know that."

"Well, you probably won't want to hear this, but it seems to me you've avoided getting serious with anyone since she, you know..."

"Cheated?"

Ellen shrugged. "That's an ugly word. But yeah, since she did that. And if this...I mean, if Fiona is someone you could feel strongly about, it would be a shame to ignore those feelings."

Wyatt raised a brow. "Have you been watching the Hallmark channel again?"

"You can scoff all you like. But I know you as well as anyone." She looked at the baby in his arms. "I know what you want. This," she said, motioning toward the baby, who was now chuckling so loud it made Wyatt smile. "A home, family...someone special to curl up to at night after working at Harper's for twelve hours a day."

Wyatt didn't look at his sister. As usual, Ellen

made the complicated sound simple. "I'm not about to rush into anything."

"Like you did last time?"

"Exactly."

"Yvette was bad news for any man," she said bluntly. "You just got caught in the firing line."

"I asked her to marry me. I knew what I was doing."

"So you made a mistake…suck it up," Ellen said and grabbed her son Rory as he toddled toward her. She propped him on the seat beside her. "You think Alessio didn't make his fair share of mistakes before he came to his senses and realized he was in love with me? We all make mistakes, Wyatt. Even a man as infallible as you can notch up one or two."

Her words made him half smile. "Fiona's a special woman and I won't have her become one of those mistakes."

She grinned. "Well, who would have *thunk* it? You do have a heart beating beneath that all-work exterior."

"Funny. Take the munchkin so I can get out of here," he said and handed Amy over.

Ellen grabbed the baby and set her beside her twin brother, younger by less than ten minutes. "Cecily told me Fiona will be here for the charity dinner?"

"That's right," Wyatt said as he stood.

"I'm looking forward to meeting her."

"Grilling her, you mean?"

"I'll be on my best behavior," she promised. "She's a part of Cecily's life now, which means she's a part of our lives, too. And the school where she teaches is one of the beneficiaries of this year's list of charities?"

"That's right."

"An out-of-state recipient?" Her brows came up. "That's unusual."

"But not unheard-of," he replied. "It's a tiny school that needed help."

"I read your recommendation and pushed it through with the directors like you asked. I wasn't questioning their need, only your motives."

"There's no motive. Just a group of children who needed a new canteen."

"And Fiona?"

"Is a caring teacher who along with the rest of the faculty is grateful for Harper's generosity."

"Your generosity," Ellen corrected. "I'm not criticizing you. Actually, I think it's rather sweet. Romantic, even."

He rolled his eyes. "Definitely too much Hallmark. I'll see myself out."

As Wyatt drove back to Waradoon, he considered his sister's words. She was right, of course. He'd pushed for the funds for the school because he thought it would help Fiona. Helping Fiona was important to him.

More to the point, Fiona was important to him. And he didn't know what the hell to do about it. He'd kept away from her in that last week with some noble idea about giving Fiona undistracted time with her daughter. He hadn't expected that it would make him feel so damned lonely.

Fiona's flight to Sydney three weeks later was delayed by more than an hour. So by the time she'd checked herself off the aircraft and walked through the gate, she figured Cecily had been waiting impatiently for her arrival. Fiona heard her daughter's squeal when she spotted her. "I'm so glad you're here," Cecily said in an excited whisper as they embraced.

"Me, too," Fiona said and hugged her back, inhaling the familiar scent of Cecily's apple shampoo, and a surge of love warmed every part of her skin.

Someone cleared their throat and Fiona looked over Cecily's head. A smart-looking woman about sixty with brilliant blue eyes stood to the side.

"Hello," the woman said pleasantly and thrust out her hand. "I'm Janet Harper. You must be Fiona?"

"Yes. It's nice to meet you, Mrs. Harper."

"Oh, Janet," the other woman insisted. "I'm parked outside. Do you need to collect your bag from the carousel?"

Fiona nodded. "That would be great."

It took about ten minutes to grab her suitcase and walk from the domestic terminal. "We thought we'd go shopping before we head for Waradoon," Janet said as they placed Fiona's bag in the rear of the dark blue SUV. "I know a fabulous boutique in the bay area where I'm sure you'll find exactly the right dress for Saturday night. It's owned by the niece of a friend of mine. My daughter Ellen bought her dress there last week."

Fiona smiled and nodded. She was being railroaded and organized, but strangely, she didn't mind in the least. There was something incredibly likeable about Janet Harper. In her white capri pants and collared navy-and-white-striped long-sleeved polo, enough makeup to enhance her patrician features and sporting a silvery bob blunt to her neck, she was just as Fiona might have imagined Wyatt's mother to be.

Wyatt...

Her tongue burned with the urge to ask about him. But she didn't. She certainly didn't want to come across as a love-sick fool pining over a man who...who what? Liked her? Wanted her? Both pretty much summed up their brief relationship. She hadn't heard from him since he and Cecily had left Crystal Point except for one cursory email confirming the date for Cecily's next school-break visit.

After her emotional outburst, he'd backed off—just as she'd known he would. He'd said she wasn't alone. However, once he had returned home, Fiona had never felt more alone in her life. Only Cecily's daily emails or text messages and telephone calls kept Fiona from going quietly out of her mind. Of course, her daughter kept her updated on his movements, which seemed to be all about work and little else. She was reluctant to admit how pleased she was to hear that he spent most of his time at Harper's. Imagining him out doing whatever an unattached man did was too much to bear.

"We're delighted you could stay with us, Fiona," Janet said, cutting through her thoughts. "Cecily has talked of nothing else but you for the past two weeks."

"Aw, Nan," Cecily complained from the backseat as she fiddled with her cell phone. "You're not supposed to tell her that."

"Well, I've thought of nothing else but Cecily for the past few weeks…so I guess we're even."

Cecily laughed loudly. "Not *just* me, I'll bet."

Fiona bit back the protest in her throat. Janet's watchful gaze was only a bend of the neck away, and the last thing she wanted to do was look guilty and acknowledge Cecily's announcement in any way whatsoever.

"Cecily tells me you grow orchids?"

It was a clumsy segue, and Fiona caught the edges of a smile on Janet's lips. But she wasn't about to enter into a conversation that had anything to do with the other woman's son. Even though Cecily looked as though it was all she wanted to talk about. It made Fiona wonder how much her daughter had told the Harpers about the three weeks she and her uncle had spent in Crystal Point. If the look on Janet's face was anything to go by, then it was clear Cecily had said more than enough. And curious relatives she could do without.

Thankfully, Janet answered her question and they spent the remainder of the drive discussing hobbies and nonwork pursuits. By the time they pulled into a parking space outside a very exclusive-looking store, Fiona knew everything about the older woman's golf swing and determination to get her husband back onto the green after his recent mild heart attack. Brought on, Janet insisted, by the grief associated with his daughter's death.

Half an hour later, Fiona was swathed in yards of luxuriously slinky emerald-green satin and knew she had found the perfect gown for the charity dinner. The color complemented her hair and complexion. The spaghetti straps, tightly boned bodice and floor-length skirt, which was ruched behind her knees, was just about the most gorgeous creation she'd ever seen and also had a ridiculously excessive price tag. Way too much for her teacher's salary.

"We'll take it," Janet insisted to the tall, pencil-thin young woman who had selected the magnificent gown.

Fiona protested immediately. "Oh, no. But could I see something else?" she asked as she touched the lovely fabric. "Maybe something a little less—"

"We'll take it," Janet said again and gently silenced her. "It's like it was made for you."

"Yes," Cecily agreed with a kind of two-against-one grin. "And you need shoes, too."

Fiona half turned toward Janet. "Mrs. Harper, I couldn't possibly afford such—"

"I insist," she said and passed something to the salesclerk. "Call that number and you'll reach my son's assistant. Glynis will give you the payment details."

Fiona's eyes popped wide when she realized what was transpiring. "I can't allow—"

"I'm under strict instructions," she explained, cutting her off. "There's no point in being stubborn about it. He always gets what he wants."

He got me into bed within a week.

Although she wasn't about to announce *that* fact to his mother.

Fiona nodded acquiescingly. She'd deal with

Wyatt later. "Thank you. It's very generous of...
everyone."

Janet patted her arm. "Good girl. And later,"
she said in a lower voice as she leaned forward
and pretended to adjust the narrow strap, "you
can tell me exactly what you've done to my son
that's got him so wound up he can barely string
a sentence together without snapping people's
heads off."

"What I've done?" she echoed, mortified and
confused. "I don't—"

"Later," Janet insisted. "And now," she said to
the clerk, "let's match this dress with a wicked
pair of heels."

And just like that, Fiona got sucked into the
Harpers' world. And worse, was terrified she
might get tossed out again when the weekend
was over.

Wyatt drove to Waradoon Friday evening. As
he eased the BMW into the driveway, the big
house greeted him with welcoming warmth.
And as always, the tension knotted in the cen-

ter of his chest eased slowly. But not all the way. At least, not tonight.

He parked behind Ellen and Alessio's hulking SUV and killed the engine. After a couple of long breaths, he grabbed his iPhone and jacket and headed inside.

The moment he stepped across the threshold, he heard voices coming from out the back and the sound of splashing water. He made his way past the wide front entrance and down the hall. He found Rosa in the kitchen, creating a variety of homemade pizzas.

"They look good," he said and moved to swipe a slice from the pizza she'd just pulled from the wood-fired stove his mother had installed to complement the huge red cedar kitchen.

"You wait," Rosa scolded, her accent thickly Sicilian even though she'd lived in Australia most of her adult life. Nearly all of those years, she'd lived and worked at Waradoon along with her husband. "Enough for *esrebody*."

"Rosalie, you're breaking my heart."

"Ha," she scoffed. "You only hungry now because you don't eat in the city." She looked him over and grunted. "You too skinny. You need to work less and eat and make love more."

Wyatt laughed. "I'll see what I can do."

"I'm speaking serious. A man needs love— just ask my Silvio."

He looked at the pizza and winked. "If I promise to love more, can I have a piece?"

"You go," she said and shooed him off. "Your mama been expecting you for hours. And *Cecilia*. Everyone waits for you."

He laughed, saluted and headed outside.

Of course, the first person he spotted when he slipped through the door and onto the huge patio was Fiona. She stood at the far end of the heated pool, illuminated by the lights behind, poised and ready to dive into the water. The black high-cut bikini amplified the sheer luminescent beauty of her skin and her wet hair clung to her scalp. His body stirred, remembering… wanting.

Mesmerized, he watched as she took a long

breath, bent her knees and pushed herself off the pool's edge. The dive was clean and swift, and within seconds she surfaced above the water.

"Aren't you a little overdressed for a pool party?"

Wyatt looked to his left. Ellen had approached, hair wet, a sarong wrapped around her bathing suit and both brows raised.

"I wasn't aware we were having a party."

"Mother's idea," she explained. "To keep the kids happy."

Wyatt spotted Alessio in the shallow end of the huge pool, a toddler in each arm, while their four-year-old son, Thomas, bobbed around in inflatable floaties. Cecily sat on the edge of the pool, laughing at something Fiona had said.

"I guess I'll go get changed."

"Good idea. And keep the X-rated thoughts under wraps until we've all gone home, will you?"

"What?"

"You know what I mean, Captain Obvious,"

Ellen said with a smile. "Incidentally, she's quite the hit. I approve."

Wyatt didn't respond. Instead he headed back into the house.

Fiona hauled herself out of the pool, wrapped a cotton sarong over her bikini and squeezed the water from her hair. Nerves set in as she padded around the edge of the pool and ignored Cecily's pleas to return to the water.

She headed for the patio and perused the drinks table.

She'd sensed Wyatt's arrival even before she saw him standing by the doors that led into the kitchen. He'd looked so good in his shirt and tie, a jacket flung over one arm, and it had taken every ounce of her self-control to remain where she was. She'd been anticipating his appearance for over twenty-four hours. A surreal twenty-four hours. The Harpers were something else. Friendly, noisy, loving…the kind of family she'd only ever imagined existed. Knowing Cecily had grown up surrounded by such warmth and caring somehow eased a portion of the guilt and grief that had lain in her heart for so long.

Janet Harper was an übergrandmother and clearly adored Cecily and the rest of her grand-children. Her husband, Lincoln, or Linc as he preferred, was a handsome, older-looking version of his son. He was quiet and caring and sometimes seemed just a little sad. Fiona had thought he might resent her sudden involvement with his family, considering he'd lost his oldest daughter, and now she'd resurfaced and was very much a part of Cecily's life. But on the contrary, he couldn't have been more welcoming. The day before he'd given her a tour of Waradoon on the back of a quad bike, showing off his herd of Wagyu cattle and the small crop of grapevines he tended to.

Ellen, she'd discovered, was incredibly likable and her husband more good-looking than a straight man had any right to be. They were all remarkable people. Good people.

"Shall we have that talk now?"

Janet had come up beside her as she poured

a glass of juice. Linc was at the barbecue turning burgers, and Ellen had returned to the water's edge to urge her family to leave the pool before they wrinkled up. Wyatt was nowhere to be seen.

"Oh, okay," she said quietly and took a sip.

"Are you and my son seriously involved?" Janet scooped out a ladle of punch into a glass. "I suppose I mean are you sleeping together?"

Fiona choked on a breath. "I can't talk about—"

"Enough said, then," Janet responded. "It's your business what you do. I just don't want to see anyone get hurt. I must say how happy Cecily is that you're here. We all are."

"You've been very welcoming. I appreciate it."

"You're part of my granddaughter's life," Janet replied. "It would be unwise to do anything other than welcome you here."

Fiona understood what she meant. "But not exactly easy."

"For me it's easier than I'd expected. But then, Karen wasn't my child. I mean, I loved her very much and she was very young when her father and I married. Her own mother had died when she was five. My husband, though, feels her loss deeply."

"I appreciate what you're saying. And I have no intention of trying to replace his daughter and her role in Cecily's life."

"Of course you do," Janet said with a kind of blunt gentleness that made Fiona straighten. "You are Cecily's mother. You carried her. You gave birth to her. That's a bond no one but a mother could understand."

"Yes," she said quietly. "It is a bond. I can hardly believe how strong it is sometimes."

"A mother's love is like none other." Janet's eyes strayed to the pool. "When I had Wyatt, when I held this tiny baby for the first time, I felt something so deep, so all-consuming. It was impossible to imagine I could love another human being so much. And it brought Linc and I closer together, made our love stronger."

Emotion tightened her throat. "I'm sure it did."

Janet nodded and patted her shoulder. "It must have been hard on your own, and being so young, I can only imagine. It was insensitive of me to say that. One day, I'm sure you'll have the opportunity to share the experience with the man you love."

Fiona felt as though two hands were wrapped around her heart and squeezing. "Mmm."

What could she say? *Guess what...the man I love is your son.*

"Karen loved Cecily very much. Above all others." When Fiona's eyes widened, Janet continued. "Yes, even Jim. But I suppose Wyatt has told you all about that."

He hasn't told me anything. "He said they had a few problems."

Janet nodded. "Karen was focused on Cecily. Jim worked long hours. They stopped communicating. To give them credit, I think they genuinely did want to make it work." Janet let out a long breath. "And perhaps they would have—if it hadn't been for that thing with Yvette."

Chapter Twelve

"Yvette?"

Fiona heard the word leave her tongue. A sickly feeling reached down low. Suddenly she wasn't sure she wanted to hear any more.

"Yvette and Jim," Janet said quietly. "A messy business. But families can be messy—even the happiest of families."

Yvette and Jim.

Wyatt's fiancée and his sister's husband. Fiona had seen a picture of the pudgy, nondescript man on the stairwell wall. *Yvette and Jim.* Was it possible? Of course, because Janet had told her so.

It simply seemed impossible. Wyatt had told her his ex-fiancée had been unfaithful. And Jim had cheated on his wife. Imagining the two of them together, as realization dawned, brought a sour taste to her mouth.

Such betrayal. Her heart lurched for Karen Todd. Her insides ached for Wyatt.

Why didn't he tell me?

She hurt through to the marrow of her bones. His silence was another obvious example of how little she meant to him. If he'd cared, he would have trusted her. If he'd cared, he would have spoken to her over the past couple of weeks.

"He's always been a closed book," Janet said with more intuition than Fiona could stand.

She didn't want her life on show. Her dreams. Her wants. She couldn't bear Janet seeing her helpless and wishing for something she sensed would never be. She was in love with Wyatt. She didn't imagine she'd get past those feelings anytime soon.

"We're not…" She stopped and denied herself the sudden urge to tell this woman everything.

Janet wasn't one of her girlfriends. She was Wyatt's mother. Her loyalty would lie with her son. "I'm here for Cecily. I have to be."

"I understand you want to do the right thing by your child."

Your child...

Fiona blinked back tears from her eyes. "I do. I will."

"And you don't want to be derailed?"

Did this woman know everything? Fiona couldn't believe Janet had figured her out in a little over twenty-four hours. "No, I don't. And Wyatt..."

"Never lets anyone know what he's thinking? Or feeling?" The other woman smiled. "I know, it's infuriating. Don't be put off by it—underneath he's as vulnerable as the rest of us."

She smiled but didn't believe a word of it. "I think I'll go change now."

Janet nodded. "Good idea. Rosa will bring out the pizzas, and Linc will be serving his infamous burgers shortly."

Fiona smiled again and headed off in the direction of the guesthouse. The one-bedroom suite had a huge living area, bathroom and fully equipped kitchenette. It was attached to the rear of the main house and was luxury personified. Every detail, from the rich cream-and-coffee-colored furnishings to the wide French doors that opened onto a small patio with its own hot tub, to the freshly cut flowers and thick white comforter on the bed, which was piled with about a dozen pillows, made her feel as if she was staying at a five-star hotel.

She grabbed her green knitted dress off a hanger and changed in the bathroom. It took a few minutes to attack her hair with a dryer, and she finger-combed it for a moment before heading back into the living area. Her feet came to a stop when she spotted Wyatt outside, standing by the hot tub with his back toward the house.

The sun had all but gone down and the overhead light made his dark hair shimmer. He'd changed into jeans and a pale blue shirt, and her insides did their usual flip-flop. He really was too gorgeous for words. After a second, she walked across the room and slid the screen open a little.

He turned instantly. "Hey."

"Hi."

His gaze traveled over her slowly. "It's good to see you."

"You, too."

They were being so polite she wanted to scream.

"Are you comfortable here?" he asked, gesturing toward the guesthouse.

"Yes, very much."

"Cecily said you were sick yesterday. Are you all right?"

Fiona made a mental note to quiz her daughter on what to say and what not to say to people. Especially to Wyatt. "I'm fine. It was just a headache. I never travel well—even short trips."

"But you came anyway?"

"For Cecily—yes." She pushed the screen door back fully. "I've missed her."

And I've missed you, too.

His arms looked strong and safe, and Fiona

fought the urge to fall into them. "Your family has been very kind to me."

"Just as well," he said quietly. "Or they might get a dose of your red-haired temper."

"What temper?"

He smiled. "Can I come inside?"

"Of course," she said and stepped aside. "It's your house."

"Actually, it's my parents' house," Wyatt said as he crossed the threshold. "But it's my home. At least for the moment."

Fiona glanced at him. "And your apartment in the city?"

He shrugged. "A place to sleep. I own some land about ten miles east from here, and I've been thinking I might build a house on it one day."

She wondered if he'd planned that while engaged to be married. Perhaps he'd wanted to build a home for his new bride? Now that his engagement was over, the "one day" he talked about was probably some faraway moment in the future.

"Fiona?" He moved closer, watching her with burning intensity. "What are you thinking?"

"That having a home base closer to the city will cut down your commute."

He looked skeptical. "That's it? Anything else?"

She took a breath, as deep as she could, and wrapped her arms around her waist. She wanted answers. "I'm wondering why you didn't tell me it was Yvette who had the affair with Jim."

Wyatt visibly paled. "How did you—"

"Your mother told me," she answered, cutting him off. "Without an agenda, I might add. I presume she thought you would have told me yourself. I'm guessing she thought we were more involved than we actually are," Fiona said and pushed back the pain knocking against her rib cage. "Cecily hasn't exactly been keeping anything a secret."

"No," Wyatt agreed. "She hasn't. Cecily wants you permanently in her life. If we were together, she'd get that."

"But we're not," Fiona said and figured there

was no point in sugarcoating the situation. "Right? Because if we were, you certainly would have told me about how the woman you were going to marry slept with your sister's husband."

He went to say something, then stopped. Thinking, planning his words. "It's not a subject I enjoy talking about."

Fiona pulled back a frown. "Is that all I get?"

He stared at her for a moment and pushed his hands into the pockets of his jeans. "What's the point in rehashing the past? Talking about it won't change anything."

Janet had called her son a closed book. Fiona felt like shaking him. "Do you have so little trust in me? So little faith in…" *Us.* She longed to say it but couldn't.

He scowled. "It's not about trust."

"Of course it is," she retorted. "If you trusted me, you'd share something…anything." Fiona gripped herself rigidly. "My God, I feel like such a fool. I fell apart right in front of you. I told you everything. I told you things I've never shared with anyone else. And you held me and said I wasn't alone. Do you know how hard it is for me to talk about my past, especially Shayne and what happened that night? Do you know that I never, *ever* cry like that?" She swallowed the stinging emotion in her throat. "From the first moment we met, I've tried to be the truest version of myself. I had to be for Cecily's sake. I couldn't keep anything from you in the end. I knew I had to let you know me, so that you would let me know my daughter. I thought…I guess I thought I was getting the same honesty in return."

He let out an exasperated sigh. "What do you want me to say to you?"

She moved forward and placed her hand on his chest. It was their first touch in weeks, and she felt the vibration of his heart beneath her palm. "I want you to say what's in here. I want you to tell me what happened."

Wyatt stepped back and her hand dropped. "Tell you what? That I caught them together in my own apartment? That I wasn't supposed to be home that weekend but my meeting was canceled and I thought I'd surprise Yvette because I knew she was staying there overnight? Do you want to know exactly where I caught them? And what they were doing? It's not a pretty story. None of it." He pushed a hand through his hair. "Do you also want to know that I had to stop myself from smashing Jim in the face? And that after I'd hauled him outside, he begged me not to tell Karen?"

"Wyatt, I—"

"You wanted to know," he said bitterly. "Here it is…I found my fiancée in my bed having sex with my sister's husband."

Bile rose in Fiona's throat. "Wyatt, I'm so sorry. Did you tell Karen?"

He shook his head. "I gave Jim twenty-four hours to come clean with his wife."

"And did he?"

"Sure," Wyatt replied. "Then a bad situation got worse."

"I don't understand?"

He exhaled heavily. "Karen wanted someone to blame."

"Then she obviously blamed Yvette? Or her husband? He was the…" Fiona's voice trailed off when she saw Wyatt shake his head. "She couldn't possibly have blamed you."

"She did," he said flatly. "It was a messy time. Christmas, in fact."

"Cecily said something to me," Fiona told him quietly. "About how you didn't show up on Christmas Eve."

"She remembers that? I'm not surprised. There wasn't a lot of Christmas cheer going around at the time."

"But why did Karen blame you?"

He shrugged. "It's a no-brainer—I brought Yvette into the family. Karen needed to hold someone responsible."

"That's not altogether logical."

"It was to her. She was hurting. After the sting had left and once Yvette was out of my life, I understood Karen's reaction."

Fiona fought the need to go to him. But if he wanted comfort, he would ask her for it, wouldn't he? "Did you make peace with Karen before she passed away?"

"Mostly. We talked. She told me they were trying to rebuild their marriage."

"Is that why they were on holiday?"

He shrugged again, this time stiffer. "Karen asked me for advice. I suggested she work out what they enjoyed doing together. Rock fishing is what she came up with." When Fiona raised both brows, he continued. "Sex wasn't it, according to my sister. Which I guess explains why Jim fell for Yvette."

"And what was Yvette's excuse?"

"Boredom, narcissism…you can take your pick. For three months she did a good impression of caring about someone other than herself."

"You mean you?"

Another shrug. "I thought it was time I settled down. I was tired of coming home to an empty apartment. Yvette is the daughter of a business associate and we hit it off when we met. Or so I thought."

He didn't mention love, didn't say he was swept

away by the other woman and had to make her his own. "You couldn't forgive her?"

"No. More for Karen than myself. My sister had a twenty-year marriage at stake. But as far as Yvette and I were concerned, I got over it. I got over her."

Ridiculously relieved, Fiona continued. "And Karen?"

"She...died."

She pushed her feet forward and moved in front of him. "That wasn't your fault."

His impassive expression was impossible to read. "It was my suggestion she try to reconnect with Jim by doing something they enjoyed doing together."

Her fingers itched to bond with him and she touched his arm. "And still not your fault."

He grunted. "Can we talk about something else?"

"Sure," she said. "I was going to ask you if I could take Cecily to—"

"I meant you and me," he interrupted. "You in particular."

Fiona swallowed hard. "What… Okay…what in particular?"

"I just want to make sure my family isn't giving you the third degree. They can be intrusive at times, although with the best intentions. Ellen and my mother are—"

"They've been great," Fiona said quickly. "If they overstep sometimes, it's only because they care about you and Cecily. I'm an unknown quantity to them and it's natural they'd be curious."

His mouth thinned and he covered her hand with his. "According to Ellen, you're a hit anyway. I'm probably being overcautious."

Fiona's skin burned where he touched her. "I can do this. I want this, Wyatt. I want to be here for Cecily. I want your family to know I'm a good person and that I would never do anything to hurt Cecily." She stopped, paused, looked directly into his eyes. "Or anyone else."

"Fiona," he said and softly rubbed her hand with his thumb. "You are extraordinary. But I raced into the thing with Yvette without really knowing her. Because I was rash, a whole lot of people got hurt. I won't do that again, regardless of how much I...how strong the connection is here. I can't deny I'm drawn to you." He urged her closer. "Or how much I want you. Like right now, I just want to kiss you."

"But I thought...when you left Crystal Point we weren't...I didn't think you wanted this."

"I backed off, yes," he said on a sigh. "Because you wanted time with Cecily and our involvement was distracting you from that. I promised you three weeks where you could get to know your daughter."

"That's why I got the big-brother routine during that last week?"

He half smiled and leaned closer. "Yes. Just so you know, I don't feel the least bit brotherly toward you."

"I thought...I thought it was because of what I told you."

His expression narrowed. "Because of Corbett?" He shook his head. "Nothing you said made me look at you differently. You weren't to blame for that, Fiona. You were an innocent girl. *Innocent,*" he said again with emphasis as he grasped her chin. "And I will always be sorry I wasn't there to protect you."

She melted, as she knew she would. He kissed her with such searing passion and skill Fiona's knees threatened to give way. So she held on, gripping his shoulders with a kind of mad desperation. It had been forever since he'd kissed her with such intensity, and she craved his touch and possession as if it was a searing thirst.

Fiona thrust her fingertips into his hair and pulled him closer. She loved him so much. Wanted him so much. And she almost told him so. Almost. Something held her back, a lingering fear, from long ago, from now. From the very moment she found herself in. *No one has ever truly loved me. Why would Wyatt?* He wanted her, which was obvious. But if it were just sex? If it were only ever just sex…would that be enough?

"Fiona…" he muttered against her lips. "I want to—"

"Knock, knock!"

A tap on the door, and Cecily's chirpy voice acted like a bucket of cold water. They pulled apart like a pair of guilty teenagers, and Fiona pushed her hair back with a shaky hand.

"Sorry to interrupt," her daughter said with a cheek-splitting grin, "but Nan said that the pizzas are on the table and the barbecue is ready and everyone is waiting on you guys."

Wyatt stepped toward the door. "Thanks, kiddo. We'll be along in a minute."

Cecily grinned again, looking outrageously pleased. "Take your time."

Once she'd scooted off, Wyatt turned back to Fiona. "Are you okay?"

She shrugged. "I guess."

"It's not the first time she's caught us together. I daresay it won't be the last."

Fiona drew in a breath. "So, you want to continue?"

"Maybe not right now," he said and smiled. "But you're here for the weekend, right? So we'll see where this goes. There's no hurry, is there?"

Fiona smiled, but it didn't touch her heart. One weekend didn't make a relationship. Weekends were for lovers. Once she returned to Crystal Point, how often would they have an opportunity to see one another? And how many long-distance relationships lasted? "No hurry," she said agreeably and tried to forget the ever-growing pain in her heart. He wanted slow. She wanted now. How could it ever work?

Over dinner, Wyatt felt the scrutiny of his family's curiosity more than ever. They did, he suspected, imagine they were watching a little romance unfold before their eyes. And maybe they were, but he didn't like their interference one bit. He certainly wasn't about to do anything obvious to encourage their notions.

Ellen's none-too-subtle comments about Fiona having more than one reason to visit Waradoon again had Alessio shushing her. Even Rae, who'd arrived late and made no apology, had cast her older sister a death stare. To her credit, Fiona took it in her stride. En masse, his family could be overwhelming…and Yvette had certainly complained about it on a number of occasions. The überexuberence his sisters displayed had become exaggerated since Karen's death. He suspected the girls did it for their father's benefit, overcompensating to relieve some of his grief. Wyatt understood, but he didn't want Fiona stuck in the middle of their games.

Because he liked her. And it wasn't simply because his libido had jumped off the Richter scale since he'd known her. Sure, he enjoyed making love to her. They were great in bed together. But he knew great sex wasn't enough to sustain a long relationship. She'd accused him of not trusting her and she was right. Yvette's betrayal still had a sting, and that sting made Wyatt question Fiona's motives, even if it were the last thing he wanted to believe. But what if she were cozying up to him simply to get close to Cecily? He knew how much she wanted a permanent relationship with her daughter. What would she do to get it? He didn't like how the thought made him feel.

Wyatt looked across the table and she met his

gaze immediately, as though they were connected by some invisible force. *Stupid*. He was
becoming way too sentimental. Her eyes asked
him what was wrong, and he shook his head
fractionally. He wasn't about to get into it over
the dinner table.

She smiled and nibbled her lower lip a little.
Her mouth glistened wetly, and Wyatt's body
tightened instantly. He'd planned to spend the
night at Waradoon. But maybe that wasn't a
great idea. Spending the night with Fiona was
out of the question. Yet spending the night with
Fiona was exactly what he wanted to do.

With dinner over, Ellen and Alessio left by
nine o'clock. Rae headed off to bed shortly after,
muttering something about an early morning
start drenching the neighbor's cattle, and Cecily
bounded out of the room to hook up with Lily
Preston on Skype. With only his parents and
Fiona remaining in the front living room, everyone sipping coffee bar him, Wyatt could feel
his mother's curiosity because she wore it like a
beacon. Seeing him happily married off would

thrill her to pieces. And it looked as though, just like Cecily, his mother considered Fiona a prime candidate for the role. He could see Janet's mind working in overdrive, planning a wedding, imagining more grandchildren.

But he wouldn't be pushed. Not until he was certain it would last. The lukewarm feelings he'd had for Yvette, mostly fuelled by physical attraction, waved in front of him like a red flag. He wouldn't be that shallow again. If Fiona had feelings for him other than desire, she didn't really show it. And with the idea she might be playing him just a little hanging around in the back of his mind, Wyatt knew he wasn't in any position to start thinking long-term. He didn't know her very well. And Yvette had proven his instincts sucked. What if it was just an act? She wanted her daughter—could he be sure she wouldn't do anything to get her? But as she watched him with her smoky blue-gray eyes, it made Wyatt want her all the more.

As if on cue, his parents bade them good-night. Within moments they were alone. Fiona remained on the sofa, cradling a coffee cup.

"Is everything all right?"

Intuitive to the core, he thought. "Yes."

"If it's not, I'd rather you just say so," she said on a breath. "Ever since we sat down to dinner, you've looked like you want to punch someone."

"Not exactly."

"Then what is it?"

"I want to spend the night with you," he said flatly. "And I can't."

She placed her empty cup on the side table and crossed her legs. "But it wouldn't be appropriate anyhow, would it? Considering your earlier speech about taking things slow."

"I guess not." As if he was going to get any sleep knowing she was tucked away in the guesthouse. It would be a better idea to go back to his apartment and stare at the ceiling. "I have to get back to the city. I have a meeting tomorrow."

"On a Saturday?"

He half shrugged and stretched the truth as far

as his conscience would allow. "Sure. So I'll see you tomorrow night."

"Tomorrow?"

"At the charity dinner, remember?"

"Oh, yes." She sounded vague, not like herself. "Well, goodbye, Wyatt." She stood and grabbed her cup. "I'll take this to the kitchen and return to the guesthouse."

He watched her leave and felt like the biggest jerk of all time.

Fiona had never owned a more beautiful dress. The luxurious satin was decadent and cool against her skin, and the only underwear she wore was a black thong. Cecily helped with her hair and she did the same in return. Makeup went on with emphasis around her eyes using a smoky kohl pencil and a shimmering gloss on her lips.

"Wow," her daughter said when she was done and insisted Fiona twirl. "Totally hot. Wait until Uncle Wyatt sees you."

Fiona looked at her reflection in the long mirror. She hadn't seen Wyatt all day. After his announcement about returning to the city, she'd spent most of the day jumping between loving him and loathing him. Of course, loving had won out. But she remained angry. He could have stayed. Even if only to spend time together. Their relationship was going backward. Thankfully, the bond she'd created with Cecily was flourishing. She adored her daughter and cherished every moment she spent in her company.

"I gotta run," Cecily announced. "Thanks for doing my hair. But if I don't get into my dress in the next five minutes, Nan will come looking for me. See you at the dinner."

Fiona frowned. She'd assumed they'd be traveling together in her grandparents' car.

"But I thought—"

"You look great," Cecily said on a rush of breath and hugged her carefully. "See ya."

She disappeared through the door, and Fiona heard the security screen slide open and shut. After checking her hair and makeup, Fiona grabbed her small bag. It was six-thirty and the party started at seven. Figuring she'd better make her way into the main house or risk being left behind, she shut off the bedroom light and walked into the living room.

She stopped dead in her tracks.

Wyatt stood by the door, dressed in a tuxedo, and looked so gorgeous it stole her breath. His glittering gaze swept over her appreciatively as he dazzled Fiona with a smile.

And she fell in love with him all over again.

Chapter Thirteen

"Are you ready to go, beautiful?"

Fiona rocked backward and teetered on her ridiculously high heels. "I thought you were in the city?"

"I was. But I'm here now." He admired her again, lingering around her waist and then higher to where her breasts pushed upward and added a generous swell to her cleavage. "You look sensational."

She shuddered beneath his appraisal. "It's the dress."

"It's you. Not the dress."

"You paid for it," she said snippily, irritated that he was egotistical enough to turn up and imagine she'd been waiting for him. "The dress, I mean."

"It was clearly a great investment." He checked his watch. "But if we don't get moving, we're going to be late. My father is the emcee for the evening and he growls if people walk in halfway through one of his infamously poor jokes."

Minutes later, Fiona was buckled into the front seat of Wyatt's BMW and waited until he'd started the engine before she spoke again. "So, is this a date?"

He glanced at her, pushed off the parking brake and grinned. "Yeah."

"You might have let me know."

He drove the car along the paved driveway. "I thought it was a given."

"And I thought I was traveling with your parents and Cecily."

"Even after I asked you to come with me?"

Fiona kept her gaze straight ahead. "That's not exactly what you said."

He shrugged. "Semantics."

"You're being a real jerk, you know that?" she said and suddenly wished he'd take her back to the house so she could rid herself of the beautiful dress and then flop onto the bed and cry her heart out.

He sighed. "I apologize. Let's start again. You look beautiful and I'd be honored to take you to the charity dinner tonight."

Oh, he was good. She got rid of her frown and sort of smiled. "Well, you don't look so bad yourself."

"So, friends again?"

Fiona wasn't going to let him off the hook as easily as he wanted. "I'll think about it. And only if you tell me why you really left last night."

He sighed heavily. "A momentary lapse of good sense."

"Try again."

"Are you sure you want me to say?"

She nodded. "I'm sure."

"Okay," he said in that maddeningly calm way

she'd become familiar with. "It occurred to me that we've got to a certain stage fairly quickly."

"And you want to take things slow," she replied. "I get that."

"But we haven't. So I was wondering why. I mean outside of the fact we have this insane chemistry. I know you want to get close to Cecily and—"

Fiona snapped her neck sideways as the blood in her veins simmered. "What is it you think I'm doing?"

"I'm not sure."

But she was. She could put two and two together. And the number she came up with made her sick to the stomach. Suddenly it became altogether too clear what he meant. "Do you think I slept with you simply to stay close to my daughter?"

"As I said, I'm not—"

Fiona's insides burned. "I don't have sex for favors."

He groaned. "I'm sorry. Of course I didn't mean it like that."

"I'm not my mother. And I'm not your ex." Fiona fired off her shots as coolly as she could. "Not all women resort to trickery and manipulation. If you thought that about me, I'm surprised you let me anywhere near Cecily."

"I don't think that about you. Actually, I don't know what the hell I'm thinking. All I seem to do is say the wrong thing to you and that's certainly not my intention. So yeah, maybe I do have some lingering hang-ups from finding the woman I was going to marry in bed with another man. And that has made me cautious… and sometimes plain old suspicious."

It was quite the admission considering he was usually as emotionally impenetrable as a vault. Janet had said he was vulnerable beneath his no-nonsense, pragmatic exterior. At that moment, Fiona knew the other woman was right.

"O-o-kay. We agree you're not perfect?"

"Unanimously."

"And you believe that I didn't sleep with you out of some ulterior motive?"

"Yes."

Stupidly relieved, and just plain old stupid, Fiona wondered if they made bigger fools than her. "Good. Although, I'm curious about something. If you suspected I wasn't genuine, why did you say you wanted to spend last night with me?"

"I'm a jerk, not a rock. I enjoy making love with you, Fiona."

Except love has nothing to do with it. If he imagined her capable of manipulating him in such a way, he couldn't possibly feel anything other than desire, could he?

Thankfully, they pulled into a driveway and he announced they'd arrived at their destination. A huge gated arch loomed overhead and the words *Mariah Downs* were etched onto the timber in fancy writing. There were dozens of cars parked along the road and more vehicles closer to the huge home, which looked as if it had been plucked from a Southern plantation from years gone by. Once they reached the valet parking attendant, Fiona grabbed her bag and stepped from the car. It was still light and she watched as people arrived from a few directions, dressed up and ready to make an impression.

Wyatt handed the keys to the valet and grasped her elbow. "Let's go inside."

He explained that what was once a residence had been beautifully transformed into a working vineyard and luxury hotel. A curling staircase led upstairs, and the ballroom was large enough to accommodate several hundred people.

"It's amazing," she said as they walked across the foyer.

"The original owners were French and held most of the land around here. It was turned into a hotel about thirty years ago and has changed hands a few times since then. A friend of mine owns it now and has steadily restored the building and the vineyard in the last five years. It should start producing wine again in the next year or so. We usually hold this event in the city, but when Ellen suggested Mariah Downs, we all agreed."

The magnificent entrance, the huge staircase— Fiona's mind went into overdrive. It was exactly the kind of place she'd imagined in her secret dreams—the dreams where she was a bride and about to marry the man she loved. It was, she realized, the perfect setting for a wedding. In a flash of a second, she saw it all clearly—the beautiful white gown, Callie and Evie attending her, Cecily in a pale satin dress. And Wyatt... waiting at the altar and watching as she walked toward him.

He was looking at her, and she wondered if he saw the longing in her eyes. No...of course not. He couldn't possibly guess her secret dreams.

"What are you thinking?" he asked quietly.

Fiona wanted to shake off her silly fantasies, but the idea lingered. "That would be a lovely place to get...well, to get..."

"Married?"

She stared up at him and got drawn deeper into his gaze. "Yes."

He took her hand and rubbed his thumb across her knuckles. "And is that what you want?"

Fiona's breath caught in her throat. "Some-day...I guess."

His eyes never left hers. "Someday soon?"

She shrugged her bare shoulders, almost dying inside. "I have to find myself a groom first."

He smiled and her. "I suppose that's usually the way it works."

If she wasn't so completely in love with him, Fiona would have laughed at his teasing.

Instead, she shook off her fantasies, managed a smile and moved her hand from his. "We should go inside."

He nodded and took her elbow again before leading her toward the door. Fiona faltered in the doorway and looked around. There were at least thirty large round tables in the ballroom, covered in stark white cloths and laid out with fine crystal and tableware. At the front of the room was a small stage and podium, and there were already a couple of hundred people milling around the tables, some sitting, some talking in groups. The men were dressed in tuxedos or suit and tie. The women wore an array of outfits, from classic ball gowns in satin and flowing organza to more modern cocktail-length dresses.

She couldn't help but notice how people hushed as they walked by. "People are staring."

Wyatt smiled and ushered her forward. "Because you look so beautiful. Relax and enjoy yourself."

She smiled back. But she knew the reason for the stares. This was the Harper Engineering charity dinner, and Wyatt *was* Harper Engineering. And she was his date. No wonder he'd forked out for the dress. He'd probably imagined she'd turn up in worn riding breeches and a grass-stained T-shirt.

By the time they were midway across the room, she heard Cecily's familiar voice calling her name. Her daughter was beside her in seconds. "This is our table," she said excitedly and pointed to a table at the front. "You're next to me. Uncle Wyatt's on the other side, of course."

Her joyous grin was incredibly infectious, and Fiona moved away from Wyatt for a moment and kissed Cecily affectionately.

"Shall we sit down, then?" Fiona suggested when she spotted Janet already sitting beside

Alessio and Ellen. She managed a tiny wave and Janet gave her a discreet thumbs-up.

"I think you have to cruise the room first," Cecily said. "You know, 'cause you're Uncle Wyatt's date. And Pop will be making a speech soon."

True enough, Wyatt returned to her side. "Walk with me," he said and skillfully maneuvered her around the room. The consummate host, he worked the room and spent close to half an hour moving from one table to the next. Fiona was introduced to more people than she would ever remember, with Wyatt quietly explaining who they were before they reached each table. From workers at the main fabrication factory to mid- and high-level management, directors, colleagues, business associates and their respective spouses and several beneficiaries, he showed no preference and simply charmed everyone they spoke with.

By the time they returned to their table, most of the other tables were filled. The lights dimmed fractionally as Linc took the podium and welcomed everyone to the event.

"You did great," Wyatt whispered close to her ear. She felt his breath against her skin and shivered. "Now that's over, you can relax and have a good time. And collect your check for the school," he added and winked. "Although, now the whole room knows you're with me tonight, I'll probably be accused of preferential treatment."

Fiona hadn't considered that. "If you'd rather not—"

"I'm joking, sweetheart. People can think what they like. Relax and have some fun."

Sweetheart. Fiona almost swooned. Did women actually swoon anymore?

Wyatt ordered her a drink, and the room hushed as Linc began talking about the Harper charity fund and explained how the moneys raised through events like the dinner was used. From the school canteen in Crystal Point to new recliners in the pediatric ward at a hospital, every cent was accounted for. Linc spoke with pride at their achievements and cracked fractionally when he announced the creation of an educational scholarship developed in memory of Karen Harper Todd.

The family was clearly immersed in memories. Alessio had an arm draped around his wife's shoulder; Janet and Rae sat close. Fiona grabbed Cecily's hand and squeezed, sensing her daughter needed her strength as Linc talked about Karen. Unsure about open displays of comfort and affection, she placed her other hand on Wyatt's leg beneath the table.

When Linc was done, the audience applauded. Fiona removed her hand from Wyatt's thigh and released Cecily. There would be presentations later, but for now the first course was being served. The scallops sautéed in a decadent, creamy sauce were divine.

"Is everything okay?" Wyatt asked quietly as Fiona lingered over her food.

"Oh, yes. Delicious."

He looked at her mouth. "Mmm, it is."

"Almost as good as that spicy chicken you brought to my house, remember?"

"I remember."

"That night seems like such a long time ago."

"Do you think?" He leaned in closer. "You know, I almost kissed you that night."

"No way."

"Way. I wanted to."

She smiled. "That's why you left in a hurry?"

"Yep."

Fiona's heart contracted. They'd come a long way since that evening. "I probably would have kissed you back."

"Too bad for me, then," he said, closer now. "You can make it up to me later," he said and proceeded to spear the scallop she was toying with. He raised the fork to her mouth, and after a second's hesitation, she took the bite.

The move was oddly intimate, and Fiona didn't miss the surprised looks from the family, Janet and Ellen in particular. She ignored her embarrassment and focused on her meal. By the time the plates had been cleared, Linc had returned to the stage and began the first of several pre-sentations. Fiona's was the third name to be an-nounced, and she collected the check on behalf of the school. She kept her thank-you speech short, mentioning the Harper family and how much the support meant to her small school.

When the presentations were over, the second course arrived. Supremely conscious of the man beside her and of the fact that they were being scrutinized by countless pairs of eyes, Fiona did her best to concentrate on her food and respond to her daughter's animated chatter. But she could feel their curiosity in bucket loads. Did they approve of her? Did she measure up as Cecily's mother...or as Wyatt's...whatever?

By dessert she was so wound up she barely tasted the raspberry brûlée.

"Something wrong?"

He'd asked quietly and she raised her shoulders. "Do you do this kind of thing a lot?"

"Eat? I try to squeeze it into my daily routine."

Fiona let his lame humor pass. "I mean these

events…the dressed-up, everyone-primped-and-looking-beautiful kind of thing?"

"Once a year," he replied. "Why?"

"I feel a bit out of my league. I'm a no-frills sort of person and—"

"You're easily the most beautiful woman in the room," he said, silencing her effectively. "But I understand what you're saying. I do this because it's important to my father. It's his night, really. He's always been the philanthropist in the family, and even more so since he's retired."

"You took over the business at a young age?"

"At twenty-four. Dad had suffered his second heart attack. So, I stepped in and he gradually handed over the reins."

"Did you ever want to do anything else?"

"Sure, I would have liked to work outside of the company a little longer than I did, simply for experience. But it wasn't to be. Harper's is third generation. As you can see from tonight, a lot of people rely on the business for their livelihood. We employ hundreds of staff and contractors, and if the company went down, a whole lot of

people would go down with it. Including everyone at this table."

It seemed like a monumental responsibility.
She'd never doubted he worked hard, but un-
derstanding why spiked her admiration. And
her love. He really was a remarkable man. Fiona
experienced a strong surge of feeling. Her eyes
clouded, longing grew, need for him uncurled
low in her belly and in her heart.

"You know," he said softly, for her ears only,
"if you keep looking at me like that, I might have
to book a room at this hotel tonight."

It sounded like a blissful idea. "I'd like that."

Wyatt's insides were jumping all over the
place. She looked as if she *knew* him. Really.
Deeply. In ways he'd only imagined existed. His
chest tightened as he recognized the intensity
of his own feelings. Every part of him was at-
tuned to her, aware of her on a level he'd never
experienced before. He wanted her. Longed for
her. Needed her. And it shocked him to the core.

He hadn't truly *needed* anyone before.

He almost blurted it out. Almost. He needed

time to process. To think. To figure out what came next.

Wyatt remembered his glib comments before they'd entered the ballroom, about marriage and weddings. She'd looked hurt by his remarks. He hated that he'd done that. Hurting Fiona was the last thing he wanted to do.

"Fiona," he said quietly. "There's something we should talk about. I need to tell you how I—"

"Fiona?"

It was Cecily's voice that interrupted him. He watched as his niece grabbed her mother's arm and gently pulled her around in the chair. They spoke for a second in hushed voices before Fiona briefly turned back toward him.

"Would you excuse us?" she said as she stood.

Wyatt glanced at his niece, who looked un-usually serious all of a sudden. "Is there a prob-lem?" he asked.

Fiona shook her head as she ushered Cecily to her feet. Now wasn't the time to explain Cecily thought she had her period. "Girl stuff. Won't be long."

Fiona calmed Cecily down the moment they got into the powder room and gave her daughter a gentle talk about preparedness and keeping a diary to ensure she avoided any unexpected mishaps regarding her monthly cycle. Once Cecily had headed off into the cubicle, Fiona touched up her lip gloss. Several other women came and went, most smiling, and one commented on the loveliness of her gown.

Waiting for her daughter, she felt like a mother in the truest sense of the word, thankful she had what Cecily needed tucked in her purse, even though her own cycle was like clockwork.

Except...

Fiona stilled. *Clockwork.* Always.

Except this month. She did a quick mental calculation.

Oh, God. I'm late.

Not by much. A few days. Five at the most. But enough to get her thinking. Enough to get her worried.

Could I really be pregnant?

Fiona considered other possible signs. Sure,

she had a few headaches. And her stomach had played up once or twice. But she'd put that down to nerves and anxiety.

A baby? Wyatt's baby?

The notion filled her with both apprehension and joy. They'd been mindful of protection every time they'd made love. There was, of course, that time in the kitchen when they'd improvised. And once in the shower they'd almost forgotten before it was too late.

But…pregnant? And if she were having Wyatt's baby, what would it do to their relationship? He wanted to go slowly. On the drive to the dinner, he'd questioned her motives. Would he suspect she'd gotten pregnant to trap him? And Cecily? How could she expect her daughter to understand? If she were pregnant, she would absolutely have the baby. No question about that. But how would she explain to her daughter her intention to keep this baby, when she'd given her away?

"So, you're Wyatt's new squeeze?"

Fiona snapped out of her baby trance and

jerked her head around. A woman stood by the sink. Tall and thin, she had raven-black hair and brown eyes—the word *exotic* came instantly to mind. Her black gown amplified her svelte body. She couldn't recall being introduced to the other woman.

"Excuse me?"

"Wyatt. Tall, rich, ridiculously good-looking and great in bed—of course you know who I mean. He is quite the catch. And the family certainly looks like they approve. I've never seen Janet smile so much. Even the frosty-faced Ellen seems to agree." She clapped her hands a couple of times. "Well done, you."

Fiona's instincts kindled and she had a sudden bad feeling. "Do I know you?"

"By reputation, I'm sure."

Uh-oh. Her burgeoning suspicions were confirmed when Cecily came out from the cubicle. "What are you doing here, Yvette?"

"Don't stress, kid—I didn't crash the party," she said, sounding almost bored. "I paid for my ticket like everyone else." She looked toward

Fiona. "My father does business with Wyatt. We have a table."

"Uncle Wyatt wouldn't want you here," Cecily said and stepped a little closer toward Fiona.

"Well, Uncle Wyatt doesn't always get what he wants."

Cecily pushed back her shoulders. "Leave my...leave Fiona alone."

Bless her, Fiona thought, but knew it was time to take charge. "Come on, let's get back to our table."

The other woman's eyes widened, and she raised her brows as her gaze flicked from one to the other. "Oh, of course, I get it now. The same red hair, the same freckles. You're the mysterious birth mother?"

Fiona grasped Cecily's arms and urged her toward the door. "There's nothing mysterious about me at all. Now, if you'll excuse us?"

"Has poor Karen been replaced already?"

Cecily gasped. "You can just go and—"

"That's enough, Cecily," Fiona said and steered

her forward. "Go back to the table. I'll be along in a moment."

Her daughter shook her head. "But I can't leave you—"

"Go," she insisted. Once Cecily disappeared through the doorway, Fiona turned her attention completely toward the other woman. "If you must be a spiteful witch, I'd appreciate if you didn't do it in front of my daughter."

Fiona took a fortifying breath, brushed past her and walked out the door.

But the other woman clearly wasn't finished with her yet.

When she was out of the powder room and on her way back to the ballroom, Yvette came up beside her quickly and spoke again. "Oh, don't get all lioness on me... I didn't mean to upset the kid. I always liked Cecily. Thank God she's nothing like her mother." She looked at Fiona and shrugged. "I meant her *other* mother. Looks like you landed nicely on your feet, though. Cecily and Wyatt in one swoop of your net. I admire your tactics. You're pretty and smart—no wonder Wyatt can't keep his eyes off you. I've been watching you from my dark little corner of the room." Then her gaze narrowed. "It won't last, you know."

Fiona knew there was little point in rattling the other woman's cage, knew the best thing to do was continue walking, but she couldn't suppress the rising anger in her blood. She stood perfectly still on her heels. "What did you say?"

"They're different to us regular folk. They're a unified front."

Loyalty surged through her veins. "Because they're a close family who care about one another?"

"Because they close ranks," Yvette said bitterly. "You might be in favor now, but there will come a time where you'll do something wrong and they will cast you out without a backward glance."

"That's a little dramatic, don't you think?"

"I've been there."

Loyalty turned into a fierce desire to protect. Not only Wyatt. All of them. Because the Harpers were good people who loved her daughter dearly. And Wyatt was the man she loved and she'd protect him with her dying breath. "You betrayed Wyatt. You betrayed his sister. What did you expect? Forgiveness?"

Yvette's eyes shadowed over. "I expected exactly what I got—nothing. From Wyatt, from Jim…from all of them. And then Jim was dead and no one asked me how I felt. No one cared how I felt. I didn't matter."

"They lost a daughter," Fiona said, stronger, more resilient. "They were grieving."

"So was I. My engagement was broken. Wyatt didn't—"

"That's enough. You cheated, you got caught. And here's some advice for you—when you agree to marry one man, you don't have sex with someone else. You're supposed to be in love with that person. And when you love someone—when you *truly* love someone—you don't betray them. You give them your whole heart and take their whole heart in return. And you protect that heart with everything inside you."

Yvette opened her mouth to speak and then clamped it shut. She looked over Fiona's shoulder and gasped. Fiona spun around. Wyatt stood behind her, an odd look on his face.

And Fiona knew, without a doubt, that he'd heard everything, and she was completely and totally busted.

Chapter Fourteen

"Of course, my favorite part was when you were wiping the floor with what's-her-name."

Fiona was back in the guesthouse. Her lovely dress was hanging behind the bedroom door. And Cecily kept talking nonstop. Wyatt had driven them home once the dinner ended, and of course after Yvette's none-too-discreet exit from the event. Oddly, Wyatt hadn't said anything to her. He'd even danced with her a couple of times when the music had begun, Yvette and her own outburst seemingly forgotten.

Of course, the fact he hadn't booked them into

a hotel suite for the night made her think he was simply biding his time. She knew him well enough to suspect scenes weren't his thing. No doubt an argument between his date and ex-fiancée wasn't the picture of professionalism he expected from her.

She owed him an explanation.

And I have to tell him I could be pregnant.

In the drama of Yvette's confrontation, she'd forgotten that little detail for about five seconds.

"You should scoot off to bed," she told Cecily as she cleansed her face in the en suite bathroom and ignored her comment about Yvette. "I'll see you in the morning."

"But you were amazing," she said with a grin. "Just think, Uncle Wyatt almost married that awful woman."

Fiona couldn't stop thinking about it. "Well, he didn't. Now, bed."

Cecily didn't budge. "So, are you Uncle Wyatt's girlfriend now?"

It was a question she had no idea how to answer. She was going home tomorrow and didn't know when she'd see Wyatt again. A long-distance relationship certainly wasn't in her future. Considering the quiet way he'd said good-night to her a little over an hour earlier, she wasn't sure he would be in her future at all.

"We're friends."

Cecily's brows came up. "Friends don't usually make out, though, do they?"

Her daughter smiled at her, and Fiona couldn't help grinning. "No, I guess they don't."

Cecily laughed delightedly. "You were right—relationships *are* complicated. I'll bet you and Uncle Wyatt can't wait for me to start dating." She shuffled off the bed and gave Fiona a long hug. "Maybe by then you guys will have worked your own love life out. 'Night, Ma."

Ma. Fiona's heart rolled over. When Cecily had asked if she could call her that sweet word, Fiona had almost burst into tears. It was more than she'd ever hoped for. Her daughter's courage astounded her.

But how will she react if I have to tell her I'm pregnant?

It was a huge leap. She had no idea how her daughter would react, and it scared her. She didn't want to lose the relationship they'd come to share.

Once Cecily had left, Fiona, in her nightgown, padded from the bedroom into the small kitchenette. She wanted tea and was filling the kettle when the French doors rattled.

She knew it would be Wyatt. He still wore his suit, but the tie was gone. Earlier that evening he'd said he had something to tell her. Add her passionate outburst, and she was certain they had plenty to discuss.

And then of course there's the whole maybe-I'm-having-your-baby thing.

How would he react? He was an honorable man—would he want to do the *honorable* thing? In her heart she suspected he would. What then? Did she dare take whatever he offered, even if he didn't mention love? Could she? She opened the screen. He walked inside and shut the door once he was in the room. He looked tense. His shoulders were unusually tight. Was he angry with her? Unsure, Fiona jumped in. "Wyatt, I'm so sorry about making a—"

"Shh," he said, silencing her. "Be quiet. And come here." It was a deliriously seductive command. One she couldn't resist. She moved across the room and he drew her against him. "Now I can do what I've wanted to do all night."

He kissed her deeply, drawing a response from her starved lips. Fiona's arms curled over his shoulders and she melted. Oh, how she melted. No matter what her future held, she would always remember the deep tenderness of his kiss and the soft caress of his hands against her skin. *No matter what.* Jeepers…time to come clean.

"Wyatt, I have to tell you—"

"Later," he said against her mouth. "Right now, I need you."

Then have me, her heart sang. He needed her. Maybe that would be enough. He lifted her up and carried her into the bedroom. Wyatt got out of his clothes with lightning speed and she did the same. They made love quickly, using touch to transcend words, finding pleasure so powerful she felt it through to her very soul. Every touch, every kiss, spoke volumes. He moved over her and possessed her completely, and for those precious moments, they were one, unified by a mutual need. Afterward they held one another, and Fiona stroked his back, her body warm and glowing with a lovely lethargy.

"I thought you wanted to go slow?" she said once her breathing returned to normal and as she snuggled into him.

"Clearly I think too much."

She grinned and pressed a kiss against his throat. "Sometimes. So, what are you thinking now?" she asked huskily and curved her fingers over his hip and then lower still.

He grabbed her hand and laughed as he rolled her over onto her back. "That I'm going to kiss you again."

"I thought you might be angry with me."

He placed his hands on her shoulders. "For what?"

"Making a scene tonight. Embarrassing you. Not minding my own business—take your pick."

He reached up and brushed her cheek with the back of his hand. "Cecily told me what happened. I know Yvette can be confrontational."

Fiona sighed. "I feel a little sorry for her. I mean, I know she did something really terrible, but maybe she genuinely did care for Jim?"

"Maybe," he said vaguely.

"Sorry, I shouldn't interfere. And I apologize for reacting to her insults. I should have walked away."

He stared down into her face. "Promise me something—never change who you are."

Her throat closed over. *Tell him now about the maybe baby.* Only, she didn't want to break the tender moment. She didn't want the feeling to end. He'd said he needed her, now...tonight. *A few hours won't make any difference. I'll tell him in the morning.*

"I promise," she whispered and kissed him with every ounce of love in her heart.

Wyatt woke up alone. He heard Fiona moving around the guesthouse, making coffee if his nose were any judge. It was still early. A sliver of dawn light cut through the space between the curtains. He rolled over and stared at the ceiling. He felt oddly at peace. Happy.

Watching her go into battle in his defense had been one of those moments in his life when the full impact of the situation had hit him with the force of a freight train.

And he knew what he wanted.

Fiona.

Time suddenly wasn't an issue. He wanted to jump, and jump fast. Seeing her go into battle for him had made it all so clear. Fiona was nothing like Yvette. She was strong and proud and honest to the bone.

Suddenly, nothing else mattered but making her his own.

He got up and pulled on the trousers she'd laid on the end of the bed and wrestled into his shirt, not bothering with the buttons. There was a bag on the floor, half-packed, and he remembered she was leaving today. He certainly didn't want her to go. But if she did, they'd try a long-distance relationship for a while. He'd do whatever he had to.

Wyatt found her in the living room, on the sofa, a steaming mug in her hand. In her satin nightgown, she looked sleepy and tousled. Adorable. He wanted to drag her back into bed and make love to her all over again. "'Morning," he said easily.

She offered a tight smile. "Hi."

"Have you been up long?"

She nodded, suddenly grave. "We really need to talk."

"Sure." Wyatt stood behind the sofa and tried to ignore the rapidness of his heartbeat.

He noticed her hand shake as she placed the mug on the coffee table. She drew in a long breath and looked as if she had something serious to tell him. "I'm late."

Late? He almost stupidly said, *For what?*

"Late?"

"Late," she said again, solemn. "And I'm *never* late."

He took about two seconds to figure out what

she meant and asked her straight out, "You're pregnant?"

She gave a little shrug. "I might be. I'm about five days overdue."

Two things struck Wyatt simultaneously. First, a gut-wrenching shock and then a kind of unbelievable elation, which sent his head spinning into some far-off stratosphere. Pregnant? A baby? *His* baby? "When will you know for sure?"

"Um, today, I guess. I could do one of those home tests."

"Then let's go and buy one."

Fiona glanced at the clock on the wall. "It's not seven o'clock. Nothing will be open yet."

She had a point. There were no all-night pharmacies within a twenty-mile radius. "We'll wait until the stores open."

She nodded and he watched as she twisted her hands together. She said his name softly. "I didn't do this deliberately."

He knew that. "It takes two people to make a baby. I'm not about to accuse you of anything."

Her mouth creased. "I wanted to tell you last night."

Wyatt shrugged. He wasn't about to get hung up on six hours. "It's okay, Fiona. In my eagerness to make love to you, I didn't exactly give you a chance to tell me anything."

She drew in a shuddering breath. "You're not angry?"

Wyatt shook his head. "Why would I be?" he asked, then realized what he'd thought was tension holding her shoulders so tight was, in fact, raw emotion. Emotion she was hanging on to by a thread. "Fiona, why would you think that?"

She looked up, all eyes, all feeling. "Because this is such...such a *disaster*."

A disaster? "Since when is a baby a—"

"Since I have no idea how I'm supposed to tell my daughter," she said and cut him off. "Since I've tried so hard to take this giant leap forward with Cecily and now I have to explain that, if I am pregnant, I have every intention of keeping this baby. How do I tell her that, Wyatt? How

do I tell her I want this baby…when I didn't…
when I gave her up?"

He rocked back on his bare heels. Complicated just jumped off the Richter scale. "She'll
understand."

"You don't know that."

"I know Cecily. And this situation is hardly
the same as when you were fifteen. For one,
I'm not—"

"But what if she thinks I love this child more?"
she shot back and looked at him through eyes
shimmering with tears. "And what if she's right?
What if I do love this baby in ways I haven't
yet—"

"Fiona," Wyatt said as he charged around the
sofa and sat down. "Cecily knows how you feel
about her. You're imagining the worst without
good reason."

"But you don't know…" She shook through a
ragged breath and he folded her hands within
his. "You don't know how hard I've tried to be
her mother. How much I want to be her mother.

How much I want her to know she's the most important thing in the world to me."

"I do know," he said gently and felt her tears right through to his soul. "You've been incredible with her. You *are* incredible with her." Wyatt touched her face and wiped away her tears. "She needs you in her life. Permanently. The truth is I'm not cut out to be a single parent, Fiona. And for the first time in eighteen months, I feel like I'm not alone in this."

She stilled. "What are you saying?"

He went for it. Feetfirst. Jumping when he'd thought he'd never want to jump again. "Marry me, Fiona?"

Stillness turned into stone. She looked shocked. Even appalled. "I…can't… I couldn't do that."

Can't. Couldn't. Not exactly the response he'd hoped for. "You can," he insisted.

She shook her head. "I won't marry someone because I'm pregnant."

Someone? As if he was no one in particular. He didn't like that statement one bit.

"You're pregnant?"

He knew that voice. Cecily! They both turned toward the door. His niece stood beneath the threshold, one hand still on the doorknob. Fiona spoke. "Cecily, I—"

"You're really pregnant?"

"We're not sure," Wyatt said quietly. "But when we do know, we'll make sure you hear about it first."

Fiona moved away from him and stood. "I'm sorry, Cecily. I know you must be disappointed in me."

She said the words with such a heavy heart that all Wyatt wanted to do was haul her into his arms and kiss some sense into her. Cecily, bless her, didn't seem the least bit let down.

"I'm not disappointed," his niece said and chuckled. "Although…I might be if you turn down Uncle Wyatt's proposal. You guys should get married—then we could be a real family."

Thanks, kid. At least someone was in his corner. "Cecily," Wyatt said as he got to his feet. "Would you leave us alone for a minute?"

"Sure," she replied. "Take all the time you

need." She looked at Fiona and grinned before she headed back through the door.

Once he was sure she'd gone, Wyatt spoke. "See, no problem."

Fiona glared at him. "I'm not going to put my daughter in the middle of this."

"She *is* in the middle of it, Fiona." He took a couple of steps and reached for her, taking her hand within his. "She's right here, part of this, part of *us*."

Fiona shook her head. "People don't get married because of pregnancy these days. I won't trap you."

"I'd hardly call this a trap."

She pulled away and stood, pushing her hair from her face. "You know, you're just about the most honorable man I've ever met. And because you have so much integrity, it would be wrong of me to take advantage of you like that. Because I have integrity, too, Wyatt. *If* I am pregnant, we'll discuss access and all the things that need to happen when two people have a child together. Until we know for sure, there's nothing else to say."

Her rejection stung like a slap to the face. He tried another tactic. "What about Cecily? You heard her...she wants this."

She stared at him, all eyes. "I explained the situation as best I—"

"If you won't marry me for *our* child," he said deliberately, as annoyance settled behind his ribs, "then marry me for *your* child."

"What?"

"Give Cecily what she wants. Two parents, together...add in a baby brother or sister and she'll be over the moon." He jumped up. "You know it's what she wants to happen. You can give it to her. You could be with her every day. You won't have to leave this afternoon. You gave her up once. You handed her over to strangers and missed out on the first fourteen years of her life. Well, here's your chance to be a part of the rest of it."

She looked so wounded Wyatt wanted to snatch the words back. Hurting Fiona wasn't on his agenda. And he was hurting her now. But damn it, she was hurting him, too.

"No. And now I'd like to be alone for a while," she said quietly.

"Fiona, when two people have feelings for—"

"Exactly," she snapped. "When *two* people have feelings. Not one person. I think it's fairly obvious that any feelings here are all on one side. Now please leave me alone."

He saw her chin go up, defiant, angry and wounded at the same time. One-sided feelings? What did that mean? That she didn't care? He could have sworn she did. Despite the uncharacteristic coldness in her voice, he pressed on. "You know I'm right about getting married."

"All I know is that my mother married Eddie Walsh because she was pregnant. And I don't want to be that kind of woman."

He wanted to reassure her that she was nothing like her mother. But she looked as though she was about to collapse, and if she was pregnant, the last thing she needed was stress. "I'll…

Sure. I'll leave you alone. Promise me you'll think about it?"

She clutched her arms to her chest. "There's nothing to think about. We don't even know if I'm pregnant."

Then marry me anyway.

But he'd had about as much rejection as he could take.

It took about sixty seconds to grab the remainder of his clothes and shove his feet into the dress shoes. When he returned to the living area, he noticed she hadn't moved. Wyatt didn't bother saying anything and strode from the guesthouse.

By the time he reached the pool area, he'd calmed down. His parents were there, seated under the annex, sipping coffee and sharing the morning paper. If they were surprised to see him emerge from the direction of the guesthouse, half-dressed, a thunderous expression on his face, they didn't show it.

He stopped by the pool gate and watched them. In their own world, together, they shared something unique. A bond, he knew, which grew stronger with every touch, with every moment they spent in one another's company. A bond that would never be broken. And they had been married for thirty-five years, through loss, grief, joy. Through it all. Together.

It was simply...love.

At that moment, like a lightning bolt searing across his skin, Wyatt realized that he did believe in love and didn't just want and need Fiona... It was more than that. Much more. He loved her. Wholly. Completely. And for the entire time he'd been trying to convince her to marry him, not once had he said the words.

And that just wouldn't do.

Fiona had no intention of waiting around to pee on a stick with Wyatt breathing down her neck. If she were pregnant, she wanted to be on her own turf when she found out. She was going home. She would go back to Crystal Point and figure out her next move. A thousand miles away from him.

She marched to the bedroom, making special effort to not look at the crumpled bed.

Marry him? Yeah, right. She wasn't a charity case. She could do it on her own. She pulled jeans and a T-shirt from the dresser and shoved the rest of her clothes into her case.

The jeans still fit. Ha…she probably wasn't pregnant at all.

Not that she'd be showing at just a few weeks along. But still… That only made her burst into tears like some kind of hormonal wreck.

Fiona quickly pulled herself together and rubbed her face. She'd have plenty of time to cry when she was alone, tucked up in her little house with only Muffin for company. But she had Callie and Evie and M.J. Her friends would support her. And she'd see Cecily during school breaks. It would be enough.

But inside, in the deepest part of her heart, she was breaking. She wasn't sure how, but the past few days had somehow blurred into a real life. *My real life.* It was as though, by miracle or chance, she finally belonged somewhere and to someone. And not just Wyatt or Cecily but to all the Harpers. They'd embraced her, shown kindness and consideration. She felt accepted, understood and part of something real. Silly, perhaps, but after only a few days, they actually felt like family.

The family she'd never had. And the family she'd always wanted.

Which was why she'd *had* to turn down Wyatt's proposal. Marrying him to make a family wouldn't be right. Tempting...but dishonest. And she wasn't like that. Besides, he hadn't said anything about loving her. They'd made love— which was about physical need and not enough to sustain a marriage. She wanted his love. Nothing else would do for her. More to the point, perhaps for the first time in her life, Fiona believed she deserved love.

She touched her belly, and tears filled her eyes again. She wanted Wyatt's baby so much. If she were pregnant, she vowed to love and cherish his child with all her heart. Knowing Cecily wasn't upset about the idea of a new baby only made her cry more. Her daughter possessed a generous, forgiving spirit, and she said a silent thank-you to Karen Todd for nurturing her into such an amazing person. She owed it to the other woman's memory to always do right by the daughter they both loved.

Still crying, Fiona collected her things from the bathroom and made the bed, ignoring the memories flashing through her mind when she recalled what she had done with Wyatt between the sheets only hours before. When she was done, she grabbed her bag and left the room.

Only, she hadn't expected to find Wyatt standing in the center of the living room, still wearing his unbuttoned shirt. He stared at her. She dropped her bag and stared back and suddenly didn't care that he saw her tears.

"I was thinking," he said quietly, deeply, almost uncertainly, as if his voice might break, "that if you don't want to marry me because we might have made a baby together…even though having a baby with you would just about be the greatest thing I could imagine happening…" He paused, took a breath. "And if you don't want to marry me even if it would make Cecily really happy, and after everything she's been through, she deserves all the happiness we could give her... If that's not enough...I was thinking that maybe..." He stopped again and swallowed hard. "Maybe you'll marry me because I love you."

Poleaxed, Fiona's feet stuck to the carpet. She stared at him, into him, through to his soul. "I... But I..."

"Of course, if you don't love me—"

"I do," she said on a rush and hardly dared to breathe in. So, she'd gone and done it now. "I do love you."

"I think I know that now," he said, so quiet, so still. "Last night...last night I watched you defend me so courageously to Yvette. I listened while you talked about love and I knew you would only do that if you loved me."

Completely outed, Fiona knew there was little point in denying it any longer. "I'm sorry, Wyatt. I didn't mean to fall in love with you. Right from the beginning, I knew it was supposed to be just about Cecily. But the more time we spent together the more I couldn't stop thinking about you, and suddenly I had all these feelings inside me that I didn't know what to do with. And then we made love and it just got…worse."

"Worse?"

She shrugged. "Stronger. But I—"

"Do you know when I first fell in love with you?" he asked softly as he came toward her and took her hands. "I didn't recognize it for what it was at the time. That day we went walking toward the beach, remember? We were talking and you were laughing and I remember all I wanted to do was hold your hand. Like this," he said and linked their fingers intimately.

Fiona's heart almost burst through her chest. "You really love me? You're not just saying that because you think I might be pregnant? You didn't say anything before—"

He raised her hands and kissed her knuckles. "I was an idiot before. I'm in love with you, Fiona. But if you don't want to get married, I can wait until—"

"Oh, I do," she said, happy, delirious, terrified. "I want to marry you so much." She looked up, still uncertain. "But you said you wanted to go slow?"

He urged her closer and his bare chest was warm where they connected. "I don't want to go slow. I want you beside me every day. All the fears I had about rushing into something again, about making a mistake…you know what? That stuff doesn't matter to me anymore. I made a big mistake with Yvette. One I can't take back. I shouldn't have proposed marriage. I wasn't in love with her." He sighed resignedly. "Maybe she knew that. Maybe that's why she ended up with Jim. I don't know, and frankly, I'm tired of thinking about it. I only want to think about you. About us."

Us. Fiona's heart sang. Tears came again. "No one has ever loved me."

His eyes glittered and he wrapped his arms around her. "I love you. I want you. I need you."

"You said that last night," she reminded him, safe, secure. "I thought it was about sex."

Wyatt grabbed her chin and tilted her head back. "I *love* making love to you. But that's part of loving someone, I guess. I love everything you are, everything we'll be together."

"Will your family be okay with it?"

He smiled and kissed her gently. "My family, especially my parents, adore you," he said against her mouth. "And will love you even more when we supply them with the first Harper grandchild to carry on the family name."

She eased back. "But what if I'm not pregnant? Will you still want to—"

"If it's meant to be, it will happen," he said and kissed her again. "We don't even have to find out today if you don't want to. I can wait. I want to have kids, Fiona, but we have time to get to know one another first. Although, I can't imagine anyone knowing me as well as you already do."

He was right about that. They had a strong connection, apparent from the very first. And nothing, she knew in her deepest heart, would ever break it. "I'll never knowingly hurt you, Wyatt. You have my promise."

"I know, sweetheart. And I want you to have a beautiful wedding—everything you've ever dreamed it to be."

"Mariah Downs," she whispered. "You knew what I was thinking about that, about us?"

"I knew," he said and kissed her forehead gently. "I want that, too. So, we'll get married there and I'll take you anywhere you want to go for a honeymoon. When we get back, I want to build you a house on that land I told you about so Cecily can come live with us, and I can drive home every night and see your lovely face when I walk through the door. And you can bring your dog and that horse you cherish."

Muffin? Titan? "I'll have to move," she said in a vague kind of way. "Again."

"Do you mind?" he asked as his expression narrowed. "Leaving Crystal Point, your job, your friends...will you be able to do that?"

Fiona wrapped her arms around his waist. "I've moved before. I can do it again. And anyway, my friends are in Crystal Point. But my family is here."

Wyatt's embrace tightened. "You're right. The both of us…Cecily—" his hand dropped to her belly and he splayed his palm over her "—and this tiny life we might have made together."

"You'd really be happy if we had a baby? I mean, so soon?"

He smiled. "We can add to our family whenever you're ready and as many times as you'd like."

Fiona's heart almost burst through her rib cage. All her old fears somehow disappeared. Along with the lingering resentment she had for the mother who hadn't really wanted her. Shayne was forgotten. Jamie Corbett was forgotten. In her arms stood her future. The past suddenly seeped away.

"Three more kids," she said, laughing and crying, too. "Shall we go to the store and buy one of those tests?"

Wyatt grinned and looked so happy it brought

fresh tears to her eyes. "Absolutely. But let's tell my folks and Cecily we're getting married first."

He grabbed her hand and they walked from the guesthouse, laughing and kissing.

And into the kind of love Fiona had always wished for.

Epilogue

Fiona pulled the satin wrap around her waist and sat on the edge of the bed. Her gown looked beautiful hanging on the closet door and she let out a long, wistful sigh.

This is my wedding day.

The guesthouse at Waradoon had become her home for the past two months, and she would continue to live with the Harpers until the new house was built. She preferred it this way. Wyatt's city apartment had every luxury but it was too far from Cecily. For now he commuted back to Waradoon on Friday and returned to the city each Monday. Of course, she missed him terribly, but they both wanted what was best for Cecily.

Muffin yapped and Fiona grinned. "And yes, it's far from you, too."

"You should have started getting dressed, Ma," Cecily said in a slightly despairing voice as she raced into the bedroom. "You don't want to keep Uncle Wyatt waiting, do you?"

Fiona stood and smiled. "It's tradition for the bride to keep the groom waiting," she said and hugged her daughter, who seemed to have cornered the market on pre-wedding jitters. "And Callie and Evie will be here soon to help me get into my dress."

Cecily managed a smile and gently pulled back. "Don't crease me," she said and brushed at the pale lavender satin dress she wore, "or Nan will have a fit."

Fiona adjusted Cecily's strap. "You look so beautiful."

Her daughter looked up, eyes glistening. "Thanks."

"Is something wrong?"

Cecily shook her head. "Just happy. And… and a bit sad."

Fiona understood. Her daughter's world had changed so much in a matter of months. "Are you thinking about your parents?" she asked gently.

Cecily shrugged. "I guess. Sometimes I wish… I wish my mother could have met you."

"I wish that, too."

Cecily drew in a tight breath. "I'd just like her to know that things have, you know, worked out…for you and Uncle Wyatt. And for me."

She grabbed Cecily's hand and squeezed assuringly. "You know what? I think she knows."

Cecily's lip wobbled. "Maybe you're right. And I think she'd be really happy that I'm going to have a little brother soon."

Fiona smiled and instinctively laid a hand on her belly. "Brother? You could be getting a sister."

She shrugged again. "Either is good."

Fiona agreed. At not quite four months along

in her pregnancy, she wasn't quite showing yet, but she'd certainly battled the dreaded morning sickness during those first couple of months. Thankfully, she was now over feeling unwell and absolutely loved being pregnant.

At that moment, Callie came into the room, clapping her hands together. "Okay, it's time to get ready. The limo will be here in ten minutes."

Evie arrived, and as she dressed in her beautiful organza-and-lace gown and was attended by her daughter and closest friends, Fiona experienced such an acute sense of happiness she had to fight back tears. *I won't cry. Not today.* But moisture quickly filled her eyes.

Thankfully, Callie was on hand with a tissue. "No more tears," her friend said and watched as she carefully dabbed at her eyes, "or we'll have to redo your mascara."

"No more. I promise," Fiona said and quickly pulled herself together.

Evie smiled and patted her arm. "Good—or we'll all start blubbering."

They all laughed, and it was another twenty

minutes before they were in the car and on their way.

When they reached their destination, Fiona took a few deep breaths and waited wordlessly as Callie and Cecily fiddled with her veil and train and then walked with her toward the huge doorway of the beautiful estate home. To be married at Mariah Downs was truly a dream come true. The foyer had been turned into an altar hosting dozens of covered chairs and countless floral arrangements. Her friends and several work colleagues from Crystal Point were there, as were the Harpers and their extended family. As she stood beneath the threshold and waited for the music to begin, she spotted Wyatt by the stairway. He looked handsome in his dark suit as he spoke quietly to Alessio, who stood at his side as best man.

And then the music started and he turned. As Evie and Callie made their way up the aisle in turn, she met his gaze and her heart rolled over. The love she saw in his eyes took her breath away.

Cecily grasped her arm. "Come on, Ma, it's time."

Wyatt had suggested she walk down the aisle with her daughter, and Fiona had felt the rightness of it through to her bones. When they reached the altar, Cecily took Fiona's small posy bouquet and gave her uncle a beaming smile as she stepped in beside Evie and Callie.

Fiona turned toward Wyatt and he took her hand.

"Hey, beautiful," he said softly. "You made it."

"I made it," she whispered.

"*We* made it," he said and gently squeezed her fingers.

Every ounce of love she had for him rose up and she reached out to grab Cecily's hand, linking them all together. "Yes, we certainly did."

* * * * *